THE GILDED CAGE

THE GILDED CAGE

COLIN WALKER

JANUS PUBLISHING COMPANY
London, England

First published in Great Britain 1998
by Janus Publishing Company Limited,
Edinburgh House, 19 Nassau Street,
London W1N 7RE

www.januspublishing.co.uk

**A CIP catalogue record for this book
is available from the British Library.**

ISBN 1 85756 388 3

Phototypeset in 10.5 on 12 Palatino
by Keyboard Services, Luton, Beds

Cover design John Anastasio – Creative Line

Printed and bound in Great Britain by
Antony Rowe Ltd, Chippenham, Wiltshire

Also by Colin Walker:

INCOMPATIBILITY, a novel

It is not for us, the staid lovers ... to condemn without appeal the fierceness of thwarted desire.

Joseph Conrad,
Under Western Eyes

For
Simon Silver

PRINCIPAL CHARACTERS

DOROTHY BLANCHARD (born Hatfield), who writes under the names of MARY ORCHARD, DOROTHY HENDERSON and IVY ROBINSON.

ROBIN BLANCHARD. Dorothy's husband, whose deceased first wife was called Wendy.

HILARY BLANCHARD. Robin's daughter by Wendy.

IDA PRINCE. Dorothy's secretary and companion.

MARK NOLAN. Literary agent who becomes a friend of the Blanchards.

MAX BLANCHARD. Robin's father, whose deceased first wife was the actress, Pixie Tory.

NORAH BLANCHARD. Max's second wife and therefore Robin's stepmother.

CHAPTER ONE

The last of the corn had been cut and it stood now in gold blocks on the shaven fields surrounding the English village of Arrowcross. At Arrowcross Farm, on the terrace at the back of the house, two couples and a girl of eleven were finishing dinner.

'Pity these three are going back to London tomorrow,' Max Blanchard remarked to Norah. 'Lionel Tenbury rang up while you and Dorothy were putting the horses to bed. Cubbing starts on Wednesday. We've to be on parade at seven o'clock sharp.'

'The resumption of barbarism,' sighed his pretty son. 'I shall include all foxes in my prayers tonight.'

'Me too, Daddy,' Hilary promised.

'*I* too,' Dorothy corrected, coldly, killing the smile on the girl's lips. 'The personal pronoun is here in the nominative case, not the accusative, a following finite verb being understood.'

'The novelist explains,' cackled fat little Norah, her Irish brogue more than usually to the fore. 'But as we're being meticulously correct this evening, shall I say the unpublished novelist?'

'Barbarism, my foot!' growled Max, referring to his son's remark and staring him down. 'The fox is a thief and a killer and he's got to be kept down. If hounds get him, it's a clean kill. If they don't, he lives to run another day. The alternatives to hunting are gassing, trapping, poisoning and shooting, and all four are as cruel as they are clumsy and inefficient. All this talk about marksmen being substituted for hounds is dangerous nonsense. I've been a shooter all my life, but not even I would guarantee to dispatch a fox who was running fast and

1

low through woodland. I'd be much more likely to send him to earth with shattered bones and torn flesh. Never forget that the fox knows more about fieldcraft than a regiment of infantry instructors.'

'If you say so, Father,' said Robin. He turned to Hilary. 'D'you want to leave the table, Hilarious? It's turned eight o'clock and we've to be up with the lark in the morning.'

'Yes, it's time you were in bed,' Dorothy told her step-daughter. 'Daddy will come up at nine to tuck you in and put your light out. You may read till then, but not that book I saw you with at lunchtime. I've put it back in the library. It's far too old for you.'

With closed lips and downcast eyes, Hilary stood up and went to Max and Norah to say goodnight and thank them for the meal. Finally, she came to her father and kissed his cheek.

'Goodnight, Bobbins,' she said, caressing him with her voice. 'If I pack my things now, may I go and see the foals in the morning?'

Robin looked over at his wife.

'We'll see when morning comes, Hilary,' Dorothy decided, crisply. 'Off you go now. Goodnight and sleep well.'

'I think you're ready for the hunting field, Dorothy,' said Max Blanchard, when Hilary had left the terrace. 'I can't give you a date till the calendar comes out, and that won't be much before the opening Meet. I'll put you on Snowball. You've ridden him every morning for the last fortnight and found him quiet and responsive. Just remember he jumps big, so hang on to his mane as he takes off.'

Dorothy's joy lit her grey eyes and spread into a smile that revealed white and even teeth. Ever since her marriage to Robin Blanchard had introduced her to Max and Norah and the class of people with whom they associated, she had craved inclusion in the hunting set and had been preparing herself with lessons at the Creaking Saddles Riding Academy in south London.

She turned impulsively to Norah.

'*Vous devez me faire savoir ce qu'il faut porter à la chasse*,' she declared, pretending to forget the older woman's request that she practise her French only when they were alone together. 'All I have at present are the clothes I wear at the

2

Academy, but I want to be properly dressed if I'm going hunting.'

'Robin will tell you what is correct dress,' said Max. 'And I'll give you a blank cheque to buy all you need from Swaine Adeney. Look upon it as a small reward for making a man out of my son.'

Norah was silent. In her opinion, Dorothy was doing precisely the opposite.

'Dilly darling, you'll look absolutely ravishing in hunting fig,' Robin told his wife, his blue eyes shining with enthusiasm. 'I shall dress you in black jackboots, fawn breeches, navy blue jacket with black velvet collar, a black bowler with a curly brim and a white stock with a diamond pin. If Father isn't already overdrawn at Coutts', he will be before we leave Piccadilly. Oh, and you shall have mock spurs and a hunting whip, which latter I shall show you not only how to carry but also how to hang, and which you use, please note, only to scratch your back and open gates.'

'I shall crack it behind you, like a lungeing whip, if you don't get a move on with your decorating,' said Dorothy, rising with the others and following them into the drawing room. 'You won't recognise the flat next time you come to see us, Norah. I've got Rabbit painting and papering throughout, obliterating every trace of Candy Dollis's daubings and the foul nicotine of Derek Comfort.'

'Your husband's name is Robin,' Norah observed, quietly.

'I call him Rabbit because that's what he is,' Dorothy answered, boldly, unaware of the look she got from the Blanchards' housekeeper, who regarded her as a bitch and a social climber.

'Will that be all, Mr Max?' the latter asked, having parked a trolley with the coffee things on it next to her employer's armchair.

'Thanks, Mrs Trapnell. Sleep tight and enjoy tomorrow with your son and his family,' Max answered.

He began dispensing coffee as the housekeeper went out to the terrace to clear the dining table.

'I wish you'd married Rabbit before I sold Blanchard Brothers,' Max told his daughter-in-law. 'Between the wars, my brother and I built it up from a backstreet business to a

3

company that earned the respect of Holland and Holland and even of Purdey's.'

'Not even my darling Daffodil could have thrust me into the firearms industry,' Robin said, his voice rich with contentment. 'I'm the champion of disarmament and the enemy of bloodsports.'

'You should have been a girl,' growled his father, making Norah's face tighten with disapproval. 'If the Second World War hadn't turned life upside down, I'd have sent you away to boarding school, where cold baths and beatings would have made a man out of you. As it was, I had to leave you behind with the women.'

'Shotguns aren't weapons of war, Rob,' Norah told her stepson. 'As to bloodsports, I can't see much difference between sending farm animals to the slaughterhouse and driving game birds over guns. They all end up on the table.'

'Where you tuck into them, Robin Blanchard, along with the rest of us. So much for your principles!' exclaimed Dorothy. '"Kill as much as you like, but don't let me see you do it" say you and your kind. Listen! If you really care about cruelty, you should work to ban vivisection and rod-and-line fishing, both of which are revolting beyond description.'

'Oh, I admit to being weak and hypocritical and I frequently despise myself for it,' Robin said.

Norah told him he mustn't. There was a debit and a credit side to everyone.

'You're kind and considerate and open-handed with everything you have,' she elaborated, aiming the assertion more at Max and Dorothy than at Robin. 'The pity is that your qualities make you the easy prey of bullies and scroungers. You know whom I'm thinking of, dear.'

'I do, sweet and lovely Norah, but my wife won't let me mention their names, not even among consenting adults. If you'll slip me a looking-glass, I'll breathe on it and write their initials in the mist.'

'Don't be so silly,' Dorothy snapped. 'I told you to shut up about them because I was sick to death of your hero-worship. You still won't accept, will you, that they're frauds and leeches?'

'Derek Comfort has been my friend for ten years or more –

4

ever since I moved from this farm to London in 1945 and rented the flat we live in now,' Robin responded. 'As for Candy Dollis, if you want to know how patient and loving she is – to say nothing of being very amusing company – you have only to talk to Hilary. I invited Derek and Candy to share the flat after poor Wendy died, because I couldn't bear being alone and because I wanted to help them develop their talents.'

'Talents! The only talent I ever detected in them was a talent for avoiding work and living off the community,' Dorothy retorted, scornfully. 'They and their kind should be thrown into labour camps.'

'Priceless, isn't she?' said Robin, smiling and blinking as he glanced from Norah to his father and back again to Norah.

'Some might say she was born too late and in the wrong country,' remarked the latter.

'I detest posers and parasites,' Dorothy concluded, all but spitting the words. 'We had workhouses and labour camps in this country before 1939 and we should have them now.'

She and Candy had disliked each other from the moment of their introduction in the taproom of The Cross Keys, which Robin called The Cross Eyes, near Broadcasting House. Subsequently, Candy had implored him not to marry Dorothy. With her arms round his neck and her nose rubbing his, she had murmured, 'She doesn't love you or Hilary or anyone else. All she's after is a better life than she can provide for herself. Once she's got you, she'll make you dance to her tune and you won't be able to stand up to her.'

For her part, Dorothy had been equally scathing, condemning The Tramps, as she called Candy and Derek, for despising capitalism whilst accepting the benefits it provided. Between ineffectually keeping house and playing mother to Hilary, Candy painted at her easel or on the walls, usually in bare feet and a floor-length dress, copious beads and bangles and a pair of blue-tinted spectacles in circular rims. Her face was long and pale without being miserable. The mermaid hair, lank and sleek and of deepest gold, brushed the top of her neat bottom. Her vagueness and occasional displays of childlike innocence, complete with little-me voice, were as studied as Derek Comfort's pose of languid dilettantism.

5

Like Max Blanchard, Comfort was a big man, tall and hefty. He had a mane of brown hair through which he frequently pushed both hands. His invariable attire comprised a large suit of Brunswick green corduroy, a check shirt, a woollen tie and brown brogues. To Dorothy's unconcealed disgust, he continually lit and relit a Sherlock Holmes pipe. Watching him coldly, she dismissed him as one of those intellectual frauds who substitute Kafka, James Joyce and E. M. Forster for a genuine love and knowledge of literature. He saw himself as an incipient biographer and had for long been 'collecting facts – umph?' in preparation for the writing of 'a major study – umph? – of Mulsanne and that whole exciting period on the Left Bank, umph?': an exercise, as Robin himself admitted with amused tolerance, that seemed limited to extensive reading at the fireside and much drawling about 'the brooding power' and 'the essential moodiness' of the Frenchman's novels. Umph?

Disturbed by the noise and tobacco smoke surrounding her, Dorothy decided at that first sighting that she wanted nothing further to do with The Tramps and that, once married, she would forbid Robin to continue the friendship. Sitting stiffly erect in her grey two-piece, black blouse open over the collar, grey nylons and black patent leather court shoes, she sipped intermittently from a glass of clear lemonade while Candy and the men sank pints of Reklaw's Bitter. After she had told them that she never touched alcohol and couldn't make small talk, Candy and Derek left her to her inhibitions and turned instead to making Robin bump-bump the table with his fist while exclaiming 'Priceless!' in delighted appreciation of stories concerning people known to him and themselves but not to Dorothy.

On the way back to the flat in Great Homer Street, she walked beside Derek, who discovered to his visible unease that she had read all four of Mulsanne's novels and, what's more, had read them in French! Once indoors, he settled to playing the Halle upright passably well while Candy served chips and saveloys and mugs of cocoa. She sat on the floor to eat her portion and read aloud 'delicious things' from the copy of the *New Statesman & Nation* that Dorothy had bought in Belsize Park to read on the Underground journey to

6

Goodge Street. Then, tossing it over her shoulder with the exclamation 'Phooey!', she crossed to the piano, sank to her hams and warbled *They'll Never Believe Me* to her swain, who sat hunched over the keyboard, kneading rather then pressing the keys, the mildewed reed of the Sherlock Holmes pipe clamped between his jaws.

'I notice they dropped you as soon as you'd spent the last of your inheritance,' Dorothy said, speaking to her husband across the drawing room. 'In other words, when you could no longer top up their State handouts.'

'Not so,' he replied, firmly. 'I spent the last of my mother's money two years ago on uniforms for Hilary when Norah, bless her, insisted on paying for her to go to Holy Sepulchre. Candy and Derek left the flat because you and I were getting married and for no other reason. You're making the facts fit your prejudices, my lady Dorothy.'

'Are they still in Guernsey, Rob?' Norah asked.

'Jersey. Yes, so far as I know. Last I heard, they were working in a hotel in St Helier.'

At first, they had written to Robin, but Dorothy wouldn't let him reply and presently the letters stopped.

'The only person you're free to correspond with is your course tutor,' she had told him.

She had made it a condition of their marrying that he cease to be a window dresser and become a sales representative, a calling followed by her late maternal grandfather, Stuart Henderson, and one she considered both respectable and respected. On his thirty-first birthday, she had presented him with a correspondence course.

'Rabbit is going to be a sales manager by 1960 and a sales director by 1965,' she told Max and Norah. 'Aren't you, Rabbit?'

'I note that you have fixed the year, but not yet the day, much less the hour,' Robin observed, censuring his wife with a raised index finger. 'I call that negligence, Dilpickle, and you shall answer for it later.'

Norah had been looking through her magnifying glass at share prices in *The Times*, and now she got up, fanning her face with the folded paper, and crossed to the French windows.

7

'It's stifling in here. I'm going to open doors and windows and damn the insect invasion.'

'We'll have a storm before morning,' Max predicted. He drained his coffee cup and added, 'It's been building for days.'

'Don't say that, please!' Dorothy exclaimed.

'Dilly's terrified of thunder and lightning,' said Robin, gleefully. 'It's the one thing I've discovered that flusters her, although I've still to try her with mice.'

'You've been so good to us, both of you,' Dorothy said, addressing host and hostess. 'Will you do one thing more to please us?'

'Sing *The Indian Love Call*,' said Robin.

'Spend Christmas with us in London. With Robin and me and Hilary. Please say you'll come, then we can repay a little of the hospitality we've enjoyed here – not just this last fortnight,' Dorothy went on, 'but almost every weekend since we married. You never let us do anything for you.'

'You took us to dinner at Bytheway House on our anniversary and you always bring chocolates or homemade cake. What more can we ask?' Norah inquired. 'Besides, you make four at bridge and that's worth any amount of hospitality. Isn't it, Max?'

'Tell you what we'll do,' Max decided. 'We'll drive up for Christmas dinner, but we must be back here for the Boxing Day Meet, because it's quite an event in the hunting calendar and my marriage would be in danger if we missed it.'

'I can't remember when I last spent Christmas Day in town,' said Norah, narrowing her eyes to resume her perusal of *The Times*. 'We still had the flat in Albemarle Street, so it's before the London Blitz.'

Dorothy turned impulsively to her husband.

'We must have a tree, Rob, with presents and fairy lights,' she exclaimed. 'I grew up during the blackout, when such things weren't to be had, and I've always wanted a tree.'

She sat back in her chair, leaving the conversation to pass her by, beguiled by a vision of her sitting room on Christmas morning, with cards above a blazing fire, with paper decorations dipping from the ceiling-light to the four corners, with fruit and nuts and chocolates in the room, and port and whisky in the Webb decanters she had just decided to buy. No

8

matter how modest the scale, she would be playing hostess for the first time in her life and to the class of people with whom she sought to identify.

CHAPTER TWO

Dorothy was as dark as Robin was fair, and noticeably taller in the high heels that she wore even at home in the belief that flat shoes make the feet spread. She was proud of her small feet, dense bust and beautiful hands, likewise of her creamy skin, which Robin said reminded him of hawthorn blossom. Her face was heart-shaped, the cheek bones set rather high, the nose slightly snub, the eyes of clearest grey. It was a hard and intolerant face when caught off guard, and it was crowned with coils of beetle-black hair.

Night was coming on and snow had begun to fall by the time she got back to Great Homer Street. Hilary had gone for the evening to a party at the Oratory Road flat of her friend, Maud Barclay, leaving Robin at the sitting room table, wrapping little presents for hanging on the illuminated tree and listening to one of his Glenn Miller LPs on the Pye Black Box that had made its appearance during the refurbishing and refurnishing that had claimed every penny of Dorothy's savings.

'Do come and join me, Dillykins,' he implored. 'I haven't had fun like this since I was a nipper during the war, when The Man of Wrath was away killing nasty old Nazis and there was just darling Norah and me at Arrowcross.'

Dorothy told him curtly to 'turn that noise off'. She had looked pale and diminished by anxiety before setting out, but her condition now was visibly worse.

'Did it hurt terribly, Dilly?' Robin asked. He was walking towards her, his head on one side, his arms outstretched in sympathetic welcome. 'Give me your coat and my kiss and sit down by the fire and tell me everything. Women are so brave! Men don't realise –'

His wife cut him short.

'Where does that woman live?' she demanded, grimly. 'The one you went to before we married.'

Robin stared at her in widening alarm.

'I don't remember,' he blurted, blushing and backing away as she advanced on him. 'It's nearly two years ... For all I know, she's left the—'

Dorothy slapped his face so hard that only his collision with the back of the sofa saved him from falling. She could hit like a man.

'What's the matter now?' he bleated, in desperation. The force of the slap had whitened one cheek and brought tears to his eyes. 'Don't start hitting me again. I can't take any more. Stella lived in Scrub Hill, Dorothy, but I don't see why you want—'

'We're going to find her. Now. And God help you if we fail. D'you understand? I'll make your life a hell on earth. Believe me, I know how to do it!'

'I've already found that out. I'll get my coat, but...'

They didn't speak again until they were heading north through steady and thickening snow in the black Morris 1000 that Sixen Toys provided for Robin's social as well as business use.

'What happened? Tell me,' he ventured at last. 'Wasn't she there?'

Dorothy emerged slowly from deep and corrosive reflection.

'She'd changed her mind,' she muttered, lifelessly. 'She thinks the police are watching her house.'

Robin sighed and shook his head.

'You know, don't you, Dilly, that both of you can go to prison? Not just the one—'

'I'll take that chance.'

'Dilly, please see a doctor. You can't be certain until you've been medically examined.'

'Shut up! D'you think I don't know my own body? I've been regular to the minute ever since I was a schoolgirl.'

'Then go through with it, I beg you. For your own sake, Dorothy.'

'For yours, you mean. You're glad, aren't you, that I'm pregnant?'

'Well, I can't say I'm sorry. Isn't it natural to want children? I love kids.'

'Well, I don't. And if you think I'm going to ruin my life and my figure for the sake of giving you a slimy little infant, you're mistaken.'

'Dilly, you speak all the time as if I raped you. As if I stole something. We're man and wife. We were together in a double bed, and when the storm broke, as Father said it would, you clung to me and you were trembling. We couldn't help what happened next, and for God's sake why should we?'

'You took advantage of my fear, knowing full well that I allow lovemaking only when it's safe. Well, you'll pay for your lust. If this prostitute of yours doesn't know anyone, I'll make you find someone yourself.'

'How can I find someone?' Robin yelped. 'How long did it take you to find this woman who won't do it? I can't ask people in the street.'

'Begin with your buyers. You're calling on eight or ten of them every day. Tell them you've got a teenage girl into trouble and she's threatening suicide. Invent any tale you like, but find someone and find someone quick.'

'Dilly, please let it happen. An abortionist isn't a white-coated doctor welcoming you into a sterilised clinic. It's much more likely to be a frightening old woman with a knitting needle and dirty fingernails. She could give you a septic womb or even kill you.'

Dorothy was staring sightlessly ahead, rigidly upright in the passenger seat, her fingers massaging the soft handbag that lay on her skirt. Anger and frustration were seeping into every nerve and fibre, agitating her stomach and making her heart thud within her. The more she brooded on her plight, the more hopeless and infuriating it became.

She rounded so suddenly on her husband that he flinched, anticipating another blow.

'Listen to me!' she snapped, close now to tears. 'You've got till the end of the week to find someone. D'you understand? Starting tomorrow, I'll beat you every night until you bring me a name and address.'

The car jumped forward as Robin, recalling the sting of her cane on his bottom, squirmed in his seat.

'Look out, you idiot!' Dorothy cried, bracing herself as they surged on through lights at red.

But it was too late.

* * *

She told the typist that all she remembered was a terrific bang, coloured lights seeming to burst like fireworks, then darkness.

'I lay in a coma for weeks. My husband escaped with cuts and bruises, but I had a variety of broken bones.'

'One would be the pelvis,' said the typist, whose record of employment included a few months of student nursing. 'It always is in head-on collisions. How long were you in?'

'Till Easter. Then I was moved to Elmbridge to convalesce and learn to walk again. I'm still a long way from fit. Doctor Goldie's last words when he drove me to the station this morning were that I must rest on my bed every afternoon and I've already realised why. All I've done today is sit in a railway carriage for an hour or so and then cross London in a taxi and I'm fagged out.'

The typist nodded.

'I'd love to make you a cup of tea, only I'm new here and they're a bit funny,' she said.

Buxom and shapely, she was twenty-five, with a moon face, straight copper-coloured hair worn short, a sprinkling of freckles and the loveliest green eyes Dorothy had ever seen. Slow of speech, with a husky voice and a north Manchester accent, she radiated honesty and goodwill.

'I mean to say, I wouldn't be standing here talking if Miss Hoy wasn't away on a week's holiday, because she'd be out in a flash, wanting to know what I thought I was doing.'

Dorothy, seated on a bench, was looking distastefully round the waiting room at chipped wood and sagging wallpaper, plain brown linoleum and one dirty window that faced a brick wall with a notice fixed to it claiming Ancient Lights.

'I couldn't work here,' she said. 'Until my accident, I was the senior dental nurse in a busy practice, so I'm used to absolute cleanliness. This would drive me mad. It's certainly not what I expected a publisher's office to look like.'

13

'Wait till you see Mr Grenze. The brewer's best friend.'

Dorothy glanced at her watch.

'My appointment was for ten-thirty. Does he have someone with him?'

'Only the two dogs. He treats them better than he treats writers. He always keeps writers waiting, and illustrators too. He says they're only dirt under his feet.'

'His letter inviting me here was pleasant enough, and so far he has paid me at once for everything I've sent in.'

'I don't like him. He's got one greasy suit that looks as if he stands it up in the corner at nights, one pair of shoes that you can smell as soon as you walk through his door and a bowler that's turning green with age.'

'He's only a magazine publisher. In any case, I'd rather be here than hobbling round garden paths on two sticks. But I'm already missing the peace and clean air of Elmbridge. I'd forgotten how deafening London is. At Elmbridge, I could sit in the sun all day and hear nothing but fountains and birdsong.'

Thanks to Max Blanchard's generosity, Dorothy's accommodation had included a dayroom with balcony. There, in silence and solitude, with a view over treetops to the glittering sea, she had written a handful of short stories for Grenze's magazine called *Winning Ways*.

He didn't look up when she at last entered his office and sat down.

'You're no Felicity Hatna,' he told her, going straight into the interview without introducing himself, 'but your work is a cut above the trash that comes through the door every morning.'

He was trimming his brittle fingernails with an outsize pair of scissors, his near-sighted eyes reduced to slits beneath fluttering lids. He asked how long Dorothy had been writing school stories.

'Since a nurse at Elmbridge showed me your advertisement. But I've been a writer ever since I was in my teens.'

She had been resident in London for eight years, having arrived with her heart set on becoming another Cynthia Justin Bourn. Writing in the evenings and at weekends, she had eventually completed a novel called *The Code of Pertinacity*, a

14

choice of title which prompted Robin, when declining to read it, to ask if it was a manual for army drill instructors. And it might have been precisely that, for all the interest publishers showed in it.

'Hand it in next time you're passing,' said Grenze. 'My reader may detect half a dozen stories in it or suggest reworking it as a serial. Anything else?'

'I started a second novel while *The Code* was doing the rounds, but I put it aside when I married.'

'What about plays? Old short stories...'

'A miscellany of this and that, mostly rubbish, written while I was still living in Liverpool with my people. Nothing printed.'

'Bring everything, finished or unfinished. I own several titles and they call for a wide variety of material. You'll be paid for anything adapted from your original work, whether or not it goes out under your own name.'

Grenze hit a brass dome bell on his desk and a typewriter stopped in the next room. While he scanned a printed document, Dorothy asked how many writers had entered his short story competition.

He ignored the question.

'Keep your stories simple. No long or uncommon words,' he said, without looking up. 'Characters are tall or short, fat or thin, good or wicked. Your stories move quickly on a strong plot line and that's how I want them to continue.'

The typist came in and looked first at Dorothy, lifting her chin a little as they exchanged smiles.

'Witness Mrs Blanchard's signature,' Grenze muttered.

He pushed the document and a Biro pen across his desk to Dorothy, telling her gruffly to sign between the crosses.

'It's a standard form of contract, calling for twelve stories of between three and four thousand words, to be delivered here every Thursday before noon over twelve consecutive weeks,' he said, returning to his nail clipping. 'Sign Dorothy Blanchard, not Mary Orchard.'

Dorothy gave it an indifferent glance, then said, 'I'm sorry, I can't study it now. I'm weaker than I thought I'd be and –'

'There's nothing to study. Didn't you hear me when I said it's a standard form of contract? All you've got to do is sign.'

'I'd like to consider it in my own home and perhaps ask my father-in-law to read it. He's a director of –'

'I don't let contracts out of my office. Sign now or take your stories somewhere else.'

One of the dogs sighed, as if he'd heard it all before, and the typist stepped boldly up to the desk.

'This lady is ill,' she declared, defiantly. 'I'm going to make her a cup of tea.'

'I felt fine when I came in,' Dorothy murmured, with her hand to her forehead. 'It's the heat in here.'

'And the smell of old shoes,' shouted the typist, heading for the door.

'An agreement with Leon Grenze is something you sign before he changes his mind,' Grenze warned, nastily. He met Dorothy's eyes for the first time. 'Leon Grenze doesn't need writers. Writers need him.'

'Perhaps we'd better forget it,' Dorothy said. 'The way I feel at the moment, I couldn't write a story a month, let alone one a week.'

Grenze stood up brusquely, the feet of his captain's chair screeching on the parched linoleum. He proved to be short and thickset, with a beer belly threatening to burst the waistband of his trousers.

'I'll make an exception this once, but I want it back in this office, signed, by ten o'clock on Monday morning, otherwise I'm not interested in you. Here! Take it! She'll give you your tea in the waiting room.'

* * *

Dorothy lunched at the Lyons' Corner House at the junction of Oxford Street and Tottenham Court Road and afterwards sat in the gardens in Wardour Street, wondering if she was strong enough for the heaving and pushing that lay ahead. Then she went into a stifling telephone box and rang the flat in Great Homer Street, not replacing the receiver until satisfied that Candy and Derek Comfort were out.

She was sound asleep on her bed when Robin came home from work to find that his key wouldn't open the front door. His knocking gradually roused Dorothy from a dream in which she was in the drawing room at Arrowcross, receiving the George Eliot Memorial Award from the green-eyed typist, while Grenze, mounted on Snowball, smiled benignly at her through the open French windows.

'Dilly!' cried Robin, astonished and delighted, when at last the door swung inwards. 'I can't believe my mince pies. I've got you down for collection on Monday.'

Dorothy had already turned away without a smile or a word and was walking into the kitchen, where a leg of lamb she had bought in Berwick Street was hissing and spitting in the oven.

'Doctor Goldie told me only last night that I could leave this morning,' she lied, coldly, as Robin followed her.

'Darling, you should have telephoned. I could have motored down for you this morning and dodged lunching with that greedy hog of a buyer from Ketter's toy department. If there's a more messy eater, I hope I never meet him or her or it. I felt like telling him to strip to the waist and cover the surrounding customers with plastic sheeting.'

'I had to leave my books and typewriter at Elmbridge,' said Dorothy, packing prepared vegetables into her pressure cooker and using the precise and impersonal diction that once had chilled the marrow of the junior nurses at the Harley Street dental practice. 'Would you mind going down for them one day?'

'Mind! Well, of course not. We'll go down together on Saturday, then drive up to Arrowcross for the rest of the weekend. Hilary and Maud Barclay are already there and have a few more days together before Maud goes to Rose Choir School, leaving my little princess green with envy. Oh, it's priceless having you home again and slaving away in the galley,' cried Robin, clapping his hands and rubbing the palms together. Then, suddenly deflating into embarrassment: 'Oh! Dilly dear, I've just remembered ... Have you noticed? Well, you must have done. Candy and Derek are staying here. I didn't tell you, darling, because –'

'They've gone.'

'Gone? Gone where?'

'I don't know. They came for their things about four o'clock. I've made some changes, by the way, now that they're no longer sleeping in our beds. I've dismantled one of them. I

17

shall sleep in the other and I've set the card table up to use as a writing desk. You can carry on using the room next to Hilary's.'

'You're letting me stay,' said Robin, with a smile and a blink.

'Go and answer the telephone while I put the dinner out.'

'It'll be one of my wretched customers, I dare say, wanting me to chase his order for three cuddly bears and a sleeping doll,' said Robin, sweeping from the room.

He returned minutes later to stand, spellbound, in the kitchen doorway, watching his wife as she, with lowered eyes and grim mouth, carved the roast lamb.

'That was Candy,' he murmured. A pause, then: 'Why did you do it?'

'I don't like them.'

'Is that sufficient reason for piling their belongings on the landing?'

'They had no right to be in my flat. I had forbidden you to have anything further to do with them. When I came home to find our bedroom occupied, with that silly woman's easel set up in the bathroom, of all places, I lost my temper.'

At first, Dorothy had ignored their knocking. Finally, after the knocking had turned to thumping, she had snatched open the door.

'What d'you want? You've got your rubbish. Take it and clear off.'

'May I have my paints, please?' Candy asked, becoming for a moment, but only a moment, a little girl with a curtsy in her voice.

'This is a bit much, isn't it?' Comfort demanded, when the paints were handed over. His fine head was thrown back, his mouth dipping at the corners. 'What the hell have we ever done to you?'

'Don't go near her, Derek. She might abuse you in her self-taught French,' Candy warned, watching Dorothy steadily and with naked hatred. 'Look at her eyes. I've never seen eyes like them. They're the eyes of a murderess.'

Dorothy sat down at the kitchen table and began eating. Her husband sank down in the chair opposite. The atmosphere remained taut.

18

'They were to leave here on Sunday,' he explained. 'They've just completed a management course at Reklaw's Brewery and they move into their first pub on Sunday afternoon. I intended having everything tidied up and returned to normal before fetching you from Elmbridge on Monday.'

Dorothy ate slowly, lifelessly, and in silence. She might have been alone in the flat for all the awareness she showed of Robin's presence.

'I didn't tell you they were here, Dilly, because it would only have unsettled you. Norah and The Man of Wrath didn't know, and I told Hilary to say nothing when we were visiting you. I don't mind saying that we were delighted to have their company for a week or two, Dilly, and I assure you they paid for everything.'

Robin looked up anxiously, expecting his wife to begin berating him for disobedience and concealment. But Dorothy had laid down her knife and fork and was nodding off.

'You poor kid!' he said, his voice soft with love. 'You're whacked out, aren't you? And all because of me. The accident, broken bones, weeks in bed and on sticks, loss of earnings and finally of the job you liked so much – all because of me. Go to bed, darling, and call me in the night if you need anything. I'll sleep with my door open. And let me repeat how lovely it is having you home again. Just wait till I tell Hilarious!'

'I shall stay for as long as it takes to regain my health and strength. Then I'm going to live in Paris. Alone. Goodnight, Robin.'

* * *

Two days later, on Saturday morning, Mark Nolan called.

'A literary agent, forsooth!' Robin cried, with his smiling face round Dorothy's door. 'Lay aside quill and parchment, Dilberry, and hasten to the sitting room. The road to fame opens before you. Mr Nolan wants you to turn *The Charge of the Light Brigade* into an all-singing, all-dancing spectacular.'

'Why can't you talk like a normal person?' Dorothy muttered, frowning at his gaiety as she rose from her writing table.

She glanced at herself in the looking-glass and patted her hair before remembering her resolve to make herself sexually

19

unattractive. This entailed the banishment of make-up and scent, the snatching back of the hair into a bun, and the adoption of a soot-black dress, black cotton stockings and black suede court shoes. Robin called the outfit 'your uniform'.

She brushed past him, still reading Mark's card, which she held between finger and thumb.

'I'll slide off to Elmbridge for your typewriter, then on to Arrowcross, and see you Sunday evening,' Robin said, while following her along the passage to the sitting room.

'Go where you like and do what you like,' his wife replied. 'Don't come back at all if you don't want to.'

'I'll bring you some apples and plums and fill the back of the car with the flowers you like to put in every room. Don't forget to rest on the bed after lunch, darling, even if you think you don't need to. Toodle-oo.'

Robin spun off into his bedroom, leaving Dorothy to make her way to Mark, whom she found standing on the hearthrug with both hands clutching the brim of a soft brown trilby.

He grinned boyishly.

'There's no Mary Orchard in the London telephone book or in Kelly's, and she's not ex-directory either,' he declared, in the loud voice he used when chiding someone. 'Your husband has just confirmed my suspicion that it's a pseudonym.'

'Orchard was the name of the suite I occupied at Elmbridge and Mary was the Irish nurse who persuaded me to enter the *Winning Ways* short story competition.'

'Which you won. Which is why I'm disturbing your weekend peace. Can you write a book in three months? I'm in trouble if you refuse, Mrs Blanchard, because I've already sold it, and on top-hat terms too.'

'Please sit down and tell me what sort of book and how much I can expect to make out of it.'

'An adventure story for schoolgirls. The sort of stuff you've been turning out for Grenze.'

'Mr Grenze wants me to sign a contract for a dozen short stories with an option on a further twelve. I couldn't write a book as well. Not in three months, Mr Nolan.'

'Lissern! Forget short stories. You're writing for money, Mrs Blanchard, and the money's in books. Did Leon tell you that sales of *Winning Ways* have hit the sky since you started writing for it?'

'All he told me was what he wanted from me.'

'No mention of the fact that every editor in town is trying to trace you? Which is why he wants to tie you down. Contracts don't exist, Mrs Blanchard, at Leon's end of the business. Coming from him, it's a collector's item, heavily loaded in his favour. I'm going to be very impertinent, Mrs Blanchard. I'm going to ask if I may read it.'

'It's on the table next to you. I'd be glad of your comments.'

Dorothy studied Mark while he read and decided she liked him. He was Jewish, nearing forty, with flat brown eyes and oily black hair that was wavy until it turned to tight little curls at the nape of the neck. Twenty cigarettes a day for as many years had made the facial skin slack and jaundiced, the whites of the eyes muddy, the gold-filled teeth and thick lips almost brown. He was West End smart in Prince of Wales check, Paisley bow-tie, a cream silk shirt through which copious black hairs and a string vest were discernible, and brown leather monk shoes.

He set aside the contract and asked Dorothy if she knew what it was that made her different from the rest of Grenze's contributors. She shook her head, being too modest to suggest that it might be the quality of her prose and the tightness of her construction.

'Your characters emerge as real people,' Nolan explained, with his head on one side. 'Some of them stay in the memory. In a story called *Walker's Croft*, you bring in briefly a schoolgirl called Sari Bair and she steals the show. I can see you've forgotten her. Look her up and develop her and write your book round her, changing her name from Bair to the more familiar Blair.'

'I haven't said I'll write it yet.'

'But you will, because you're smiling; and may I say that you're a very beautiful woman, Mrs Blanchard, smiling or otherwise? Your publisher is Sandrew Morath,' Mark went on, expansively, 'and your editor is Eddie Lombard. How quickly can you let me have three chapters and a synopsis? The sooner I have them, the sooner Eddie can open discussions with an illustrator.'

21

Sandrew Morath! They were Cynthia Justin Bourn's publishers.

'But what about Mr Grenze?'

'Leave Leon to me. He can have his short stories, but not until your book is reprinting and then at ten times the pittance he's offering here.'

'If he had been pleasant with me, Mr Nolan, I wouldn't even listen to you.'

'He's used to dealing with hacks, Mrs Orchard, but he'll realise on Monday morning that he was foolish to treat you like one,' Mark said, rising as he slipped the agreement into an inside pocket. 'I'll leave you now to sharpen your pencil. Aim at forty thousand words, keep the action brisk, and don't ever write down to your readers, because youngsters are quick to sense condescension and they won't forgive you for it.'

He drove away in his elderly Ford Pilot, wondering how hard it was going to be to persuade Eddie Lombard to buy an unwritten book on the strength of a handful of short stories.

Dorothy, meanwhile, returned to her writing table, amused by the novelty of the situation and just a little sorry that she wouldn't see the green-eyed girl again.

CHAPTER THREE

Dorothy took nearly four months to write that first Mary Orchard book, taking greater pains with its style and development than she was to take over the score or so of similar books that followed its success. Without consulting her, Eddie Lombard made minor alterations to the text and changed the title from *Much Ado at Walker's Croft* to *Fun and Games at Walker's Croft*.

'It has a jollier ring,' said Hilary, when Dorothy asked her opinion of Eddie's preference.

'That's what Mr Nolan says. I was angry at first that Mr Lombard or one of his hirelings had mauled my work, but I'm too embroiled in my second book to let it bother me now.'

'You're making money, Dilly. That's all that matters,' said Robin. Then, seeing she was hurt by the comment, he added, 'It's what you say yourself, darling.'

He turned the Morris 1000 into the open gateway of Arrowcross Farm and continued up the long drive, calling out 'Merry Christmas!' to Arran and Blanch Clark as the car passed their cottage. Arran was shovelling thick snow on to the small front garden, where Blanch was building a snowman.

'Phew! We're late, Mrs Trapnell,' Dorothy said, entering the kitchen ahead of her husband and stepdaughter. 'The roads are atrocious once you leave London.'

'Winter came so suddenly,' the housekeeper answered, with her customary cheerfulness. 'Come into the warmth and have some coffee. Mrs Blanchard is out exercising Merlin and Mr Max is in bed nursing a heavy cold. I'm about to take him some iced orange juice.'

23

'I'll take it, Nellie,' said Hilary. 'Are you sure he wouldn't rather have brandy and lovage?'

'I expect he had his share of good cheer last night,' Dorothy said. 'Did the party go off well, Mrs Trapnell? No one failed to get here through the drifts?'

'It takes more than snow to daunt the sort of people who come to Arrowcross,' replied the housekeeper, contentedly. 'Shall we say their spirit is equalled only by their capacity for enjoyment? I catered for twenty-two and twenty-two came. It was turned three this morning before the last one left, but I'll bet they were all out riding by ten o'clock, Christmas Day or no Christmas Day.'

Robin told his wife and Hilary to go and talk to Max while he got the cases out of the car and put them in their bedrooms.

'I'll serve tea in the drawing room at five,' said Mrs Trapnell. 'By then, Mrs Blanchard will be back with Merlin.'

Max was propped up in bed, reading *Horse & Hound* and noisily blowing his nose. He was a man in his sixties. Large ears, flat against the sides of the head, supported horn rimmed spectacles. His hair was silver and still plentiful, his face square with blue eyes, sound teeth and a double chin. It was a face that could be frightening. It was a face that could also break into an almost square smile and shine with good humour.

'I'm as bright as my fire now I've got you and Hilary to look at,' he said, answering Dorothy's opening question. 'Otherwise, full of snot and misery. I don't often get a cold, but when I do it's worth waiting for. This one has been trying to find a way in for days, and last night it succeeded.'

'I do love your charmers, Panie Bracie,' Hilary declared, joyously, using her word for pyjamas and her nickname for her grandfather. 'They're the first tartan ones I've seen. Which is your clan?'

'The MacBlanchard, and our battle cry is "Gertcha!" A birthday present from Aunt Norah,' Max explained. He turned to Dorothy, whose birthday, the eleventh of December, was the same as his. 'In case you've forgotten, Dilly, Christmas dinner is eaten on Christmas Eve in the clan MacBlanchard, as it is in France, and presents are not exchanged between grown-ups.

24

But we maintain the tradition for the youngsters.' He nodded with amusement at Dorothy's 'uniform' and broadened his Lancashire accent to exclaim, 'Ee, lass, ya luck as if ya gooin' to a funeral. Are these the writing clothes Robin has been telling us about?'

Hilary would like to have revealed that a recent visitor to Great Homer Street had taken Dorothy for the housemaid, but her father had taught her never to embarrass anyone in the presence of others.

'I've brought something less forbidding to change into, knowing how much you appreciate feminine elegance, Max,' Dorothy assured him.

'Well, we like a bit of colour, don't we, Hilary? Eh, just you wait till you see your Christmas present from Aunt Norah and me. No use looking on the tree in the drawing room. Too big for that.'

'Tell your grandfather what you got from Daddy and me this morning, Hilary.'

'A new recorder. I'm going to ask Aunt Norah if she'll accompany me at the piano after dinner.'

'I shall keep this door wide open, Hilary, so as not to miss a note of *A Hundred Pipers*. You *will* play that for me, won't you?'

'And perhaps Rubenstein's *Melody In F*,' suggested Dorothy, smiling fondly at Hilary. 'You play it divinely, on the piano as well as on the recorder.'

'About tomorrow, Dilly,' Max said. 'Three consecutive nights of hard frost mean hunting is cancelled. If we get the promised thaw tonight, OK – we turn out. If not, my dear, you and Snowball will have to be content with a little exercise along the lanes.'

'I'll keep my fingers crossed, Max, because it's a treat I've been looking forward to for a long time. But will you be joining us?'

He shook his head.

'Not a hope. I'm running a temperature and it would be most unwise. Pity. I haven't missed a Boxing Day Meet for years and I know I would have been proud of you. You've brought hunting clothes?'

Dorothy nodded and rose. She had recently resumed her

lessons at the Creaking Saddles Riding Academy, but she hadn't followed hounds since before the road accident.

'I must unpack and change,' she said. 'I can hear Rabbit clumping about with suitcases.'

'I'll stay home and keep you company, Panie Bracie, if the others go hunting,' Hilary told Max. 'I've brought my sewing and I can work up here.'

'I'm teaching her to embroider,' Dorothy said. 'With her small hands and supple fingers, she'll soon put me to shame.'

She left the room as her husband came in.

* * *

She unpacked, carefully putting everything in its place, then released her long ebony-black hair from the prim little bun that had become habitual, brushed it out and took it up with combs and pins. She changed then into nylons the colour of smoked glass, a Brahman-blue tailored suit, navy blue suede court shoes and a matching linen blouse open at the neck and with the collar outside her jacket. She had finished scenting herself and was putting in drop earrings when Robin entered.

'Hello! This is quite like old times,' he began, heartily.

His wife, with her back to him, was in the shadow created by the sloping roof.

'I assure you it isn't going to be,' she retorted, thinking he was referring to the double bed. 'You're going to sleep on the floor.'

'What shall I use for bedding? Straw or peat?'

'Use whatever you like. I'm only concerned with what you're *not* going to do, and that includes watching me undress. At bedtime, I'll say goodnight first. You follow after half an hour.'

'I'll borrow Nellie's egg timer and have it on the arm of my chair.'

Dorothy turned round and began walking towards the open door. Such was the smallness of the room and the quantity of furniture that she had to brush past him.

He caught his breath.

'Oh, you're lovely!' he breathed, seeing her now in full daylight. 'You're absolutely lovely.'

His hand went out involuntarily to stop her, but she thrust

him aside in sudden fury and slapped his face – the first time she had struck him since the night of the accident. And in that same moment, Hilary appeared in the doorway, her eyes wide with outrage.

'Why did you hit my daddy?' she demanded, indignantly.

'Don't dare question me,' Dorothy snapped, pointing with a rigid right arm at the landing. 'Go to your room at once and change into your new dress. Go on!'

She followed the resentful girl as far as the door of her bedroom, then continued down the stairs, in no doubt that Hilary would immediately return to her father to question and commiserate and call down curses on the aggressor. Hilary knew nothing of the slappings and canings that had gone before. Only the sadist and her victim knew about those, and Dorothy had more than once used the threat of greater humiliation to overcome her husband's resistance. 'If you won't bend over, I'll knock you about in front of your daughter,' she would shout, holding her cane over him.

She went into the drawing room and looked through the French windows at the snowscape beyond. The hard blue sky of the winter afternoon was ablaze with the colours of the setting sun – jade, orange, slate grey, silver, palest gold – and the snow on the distant hills had turned pink.

She heard the outer door of the kitchen open and close, then Mrs Trapnell's voice saying: 'Miss Dorothy is in the drawing room, Mrs Blanchard, and the others are still upstairs.'

'I'll take these boots off, then go up,' Norah answered. 'I've told the new groom to go home once she's seen to Merlin. Her name's Camilla, by the way. Will you slip across the yard after she's left and check she's locked up and let the dogs out? I need a hot bath more than anything at the moment.'

'Certainly, Mrs Blanchard. Peggy's coming in from the village to serve dinner, but I'll leave everything ready for her and she'll come in each morning at ten while I'm away.'

'Have a nice break, Mrs Trapnell, and thank you for last night's extra effort.'

Without a glance at the half-open door of the drawing room, Norah passed along the hall and on up the stairs, padding along in thick-knit woollen socks.

Dorothy's bright greeting died within her.

'Oh, be that way!' she muttered, caustically.

She switched lamps on and stirred the log fire before sitting down in one of the armchairs, crossing her chorus-girl legs and attempting to read *Country Life*. But she couldn't concentrate. Her grey eyes turned instead to the hundreds of books that lined one entire wall, and from there to the soft leather and mellow wood of antique furniture, the browns and golds of curtains and upholstery, the hunting scenes in gilt frames, the black Steinway grand, and the cream carpet that featured rock plants, alpines and garden flowers within an overall trellis design. A time would come when Dorothy would create a similar setting for herself, albeit in a smaller space and on a less opulent scale.

The warmth of the room lulled her into a sleep from which the arrival of Hilary and Robin presently roused her. A tea trolley at her side indicated that Mrs Trapnell had been and gone.

'*La Châtelaine* will keep to her room till dinner,' he announced, meaning Norah, buoyantly. 'Her clubroot has flared up again and she must needs soak her head in a solution of kerosene and permanganate of potash. What's for tea, kiddo? Cherry cake. Priceless!'

'Does anyone object if I play the piano?' Hilary asked. 'I need a little practice before this evening.'

'We'd love to hear you play, so long as you don't mind our talking quietly,' Dorothy responded. 'And how very pretty you look, Hilary! You're going to break a lot of hearts when you're older.'

Hilary was wearing the flared dress of bronze silk with a cream rose at the bodice that Dorothy had helped her choose. She had her late mother's rich brown hair, worn straight and with a fringe, and (that most rare of inheritances) golden eyes.

'We went to see her Christmas present while you were in the land of Nod, Dilly,' said Robin, clearly sharing his daughter's pleasure.

'His name's Harry, he's off four and a strawberry roan,' Hilary said, smiling at her music as she began to play Robin's favourite, *Kiss Me Again*. 'I can't wait till tomorrow.'

28

'She'll be busy at first light with dandy brush and curry comb. The maternal instinct,' said Robin. He nodded at his wife and added: 'Something you lack.'

'You know a lot about horseflesh for a man who never rides and who disapproves of the chase,' she remarked.

'I spent the Second World War here, don't forget.'

'Oh, of course. You were a conscientious objector.'

'There's nothing to be ashamed of in that, Dilly,' said Robin.

'Did I say there was?'

'What else could you have done, Bobbins, apart from farm work?' Hilary asked. 'Maud Barclay says COs were sometimes sent to prison for their beliefs.'

'The tribunal offered me agriculture or coal mining. I'd never have survived down a pit – not with my slight build and tendency to asthma. I learnt to plough behind heavy horses, make hay, lift potatoes, and play darts with Land Army girls at The Farmer's Arms. None of which pleased Panie Bracie. I can see him now, home on leave, in khaki with captain's pips and a swagger stick, standing in this room and looking at me as if I'd fouled the carpet.'

Max had bought Arrowcross Farm in 1929, leasing all save the house to Arran and Blanch Clark. He wanted it partly for the shooting but mainly for the relief that country air would bring to his invalid first wife, the former actress Pixie Tory. Emotionally dependent upon their only child, himself a weakling, she had kept Robin at her side until her death some ten years later. Max, meanwhile, had based himself in London, at the flat over Blanchard Brothers' showroom in Albemarle Street, motoring down to Arrowcross at weekends and travelling extensively in search of orders.

'France and Germany mostly,' Robin answered, in reply to Dorothy's question. 'He didn't like me enough ever to take me with him, but he was very successful nevertheless. Panie Bracie is like you. He can be brutal and unbearable, yet utterly charming if he wants something.'

'Max is a man of wide experience and I love to hear him talk. He's met some fascinating people in his time,' Dorothy remarked. 'Sir Henry Royce, Jim Mollison, the racehorse trainer Lennie Menzies, Isadora Duncan...'

'Lord Beaverbrook, Henry Birkin, Laval. He met Laval at a reception at the British Embassy in Paris,' said Robin. 'Norah says he should write his memoirs now that he's more or less retired from business. Personally, I can't stomach most of what he stands for. He even finds things to admire in Hitler and his disgusting Nazis. Has he told you he met Hitler? In Leipzig, I think it was.'

'Hitler got rid of a lot of people,' Dorothy remarked, approvingly. 'It's the destruction of property I can't forgive him for. Lovely old cities, some of them dating from Roman times or even earlier, bombed to powder by him or because of him. People are ten a penny, but not beautiful buildings and works of art.'

Hilary stopped playing with a sudden thump and glowered across the room at her stepmother.

'Hitler was horrible,' she said, stoutly. 'Anyone who admires him is inhuman. Maud's parents have television in their flat and we saw Hitler once, raving and shouting, and Maud's father, who was on Winston Churchill's staff during the war, said Hitler was an agent of the devil who somehow got through the net.'

Robin agreed, smiling his approval at Hilary, then moved the talk onto safer ground by asking his wife if she knew that Max and Norah had met in France.

She did.

'They sometimes told me a little about themselves when they came to see me at Elmbridge. We used to sit in the gardens or on my balcony, having afternoon tea in the sun and watching the yachts out at sea. Norah told me she had been married to Desmond Denise, the Paris couturier, and at one time they lived in the same apartment block as Charles Trenet. When Desmond died, she went to Cluny to live with his sister, who had a very select hotel there – *trié sur le volet*, as Norah put it.'

'You have a good memory,' Robin said.

'I have a novelist's memory. I remember the odds and ends that give verisimilitude to stories. Max sometimes stayed at the hotel.'

'Max always stayed at the hotel,' Robin corrected. He glanced at Hilary, who had resumed playing, then winked at

Dorothy. 'And sometimes Norah stayed at Albemarle Street – when my mother was still alive and living here with me. But not a word!'

He jumped up as Norah appeared on the topmost of the two shallow steps that led down to the drawing room.

'*La Châtelaine!*' he cried, in joyful greeting. '*Bon soir, Madame la Châtelaine. Vos enfants vous attendent.*'

* * *

Norah was short and plump, with lustrous dark eyes, sparse hair dyed black, and evidence of an Irish childhood in her educated voice. Her smile was her most engaging feature, although frequently marred by smears of lipstick on the upper incisors.

She had insinuated herself into a black satin dress that was too tight and too short for her. With it, she wore a white silk sash, an excessive amount of jewellery, and soft black pumps peppered with sequins. All in all, and most uncharacteristically, she looked like an old tart.

Dorothy hastened to meet her.

'I love your dress – and what exquisite pearls, Norah!' she began. 'Has your headache gone away?'

She hesitated between kissing Norah's cheek and shaking her hand and ended up doing neither.

'I didn't know I had one,' Norah said, looking over Dorothy's head at Robin and Hilary and smiling at them. 'I've told Peggy she can serve dinner. *Venez, les grands! A table!*'

'*Oui, petite Maman,*' cried Hilary. '*On vous suit.*'

In the dining room, the soft light from six tall candles fell on polished rosewood, old silver, Tutbury crystal and two matched Elkington carpets laid end to fringed end.

Soup was followed by wild goose in cider, with game chips, watercress, halved oranges, and red cabbage cooked with apple and vinegar. Like Dorothy, Mrs Trapnell was a cook who brought love and imagination to every dish she prepared.

'I'd all but forgotten what you look like,' Norah told Dorothy, moving a candlestick aside to get a better view of her. 'It's so long since you've been to Arrowcross that we were wondering if we'd offended you in some way.'

'I'm sorry, Norah. I must seem terribly ungrateful after all you and Max have done for me. I assure you that's not so. The fact is that since I came out of Elmbridge, I've been under constant pressure from my agent. I was writing till two o'clock this morning and I'll have to be back at my desk as soon as we get home tomorrow night.'

'We hardly see her,' Robin confirmed. 'Do we, Hilarious?'

'And of course when she's made enough money from her books, you won't see her at all,' stated Norah, acidly. Then, to Dorothy: 'What's this about leaving Rob and Hilary and going to live in France on your own?'

Robin lowered his eyes in time to escape Dorothy's blistering glare.

'That was said in the heat of the moment, when I was upset and angry and very tired,' she explained, in a tight and muted voice. 'I'm surprised my husband chose to include it in his tittle-tattle. Things have changed a lot, Norah, since that moment, thanks to the patience and understanding of Robin and Hilary. We're getting along very smoothly, the three of us. I'm helping Hilary with her French and English and, to please me, Robin has picked up again on his salesmanship correspondence course. Give Hilary a little wine, Robin. She's old enough to at least taste it.'

'OK. Some for you, Dilly?'

'Not for me.'

'Not even at Christmas?'

'Not even at Christmas.'

'Oh, come on! Let your hair down, my lady Dorothy,' Robin said. 'No. On second thoughts, don't. I love you with it piled on top of your head. Pray God I'm witnessing the first step in a return to your former glory. With luck, we shall see you once again in silk and lace and all the other things that make women irresistible.'

'That wine *is* strong, Bobbins!' exclaimed Hilary.

'Tomorrow's Meet is a lawn Meet and we're going out with the West Property Hunt, so you're twice blessed,' Norah told Dorothy. 'Provided, that is, we have a thaw before morning. If we don't, no hunt. The ground will be too hard.'

'What's up with the Arrowcross Hunt, Aunt Norah?' Hilary asked.

'Hounds have the cough, dear, like Panie Bracie, as you call him. Count yourself lucky to be invited, Dorothy. It's a privilege even for me, and especially so on Boxing Day, when all hands and the cook want to follow hounds.'

'Is it just thee and me? What about Arran and Blanch?' Dorothy asked.

'Not invited,' declared Norah. 'Max was coming, obviously, but not now.'

Robin increased his wife's discomfort with the warning that she would have to watch her Ps and Qs, and watch them very carefully.

'The Arrowcross is a farmers' hunt, but the West Property is haw-haw jaw-jaw,' he explained. 'The Master of Foxhounds is Sir Willoughby Fordyce-Fizzbottle, QC, MP, JP and Keeper of the Royal Buckets. He's eight feet tall, wears a patched suit that's been in the family for generations and has a voice you can hear in the next county.'

'Such nonsense!' cackled Norah, suddenly sounding very Irish. 'Sir William is charming.'

'He was wonderful to me at the point-to-point,' Hilary added. 'He complimented me on my hands.'

'The Meet is at Netherton House, Rob, so you'll be able to feast your eyes on Amanda Berriman again,' said Norah.

Robin briskly rubbed his palms together.

'I likes Amanda, I does,' he confirmed. 'What time d'you want to be there? After I've delivered you and Dilly, I'll follow the Field with the box to save you posting back to Amanda's after you've said goodnight. Besides, the lane outside Netherton House is too narrow to leave it and the Land Rover there all day. I'll have the bobby on my tail again.'

'I'm wondering if my riding is up to standard,' Dorothy said, unable to keep anxiety out of her voice and face. 'What do you think, Norah?'

'How should I know?' Norah demanded, fiercely, 'when we've seen neither hide nor hair of you for nearly eighteen months.'

'You'll be all right,' said Robin. 'You hunted well before your accident and you'll hunt well tomorrow. Just keep your nerve. That's all.'

'What does your teacher say at Creaking Saddles?' Norah

demanded, relishing Dorothy's deepening blush without appearing to do so.

'She seems to think I'm OK. She promoted me to Leading File last Saturday.'

'Well, then! There's your answer,' Norah concluded. 'More pudding, Rob? Hilary? I'll tell Peggy to serve coffee in the drawing room, then she can slip up and see if Max wants anything.'

'I'll go, Norah. I've got to go upstairs anyway,' said Dorothy, only too glad to get out of the room.

She was on the landing when the sound of water trickling into the gutters above the low windows made her pause and bite her lower lip.

CHAPTER FOUR

Not until the horses were unboxed at the Meet did Dorothy realise that she was not to ride Snowball. Norah's mount, Merlin, clumped down the ramp first, then came this big bay, impeccably turned out from plaited mane to oiled hooves, and with the most bad-tempered eye Dorothy had ever seen.

He was new to her husband also. The box had been loaded and closed by Camilla before Robin and his two passengers had taken their seats in the Land Rover for the journey from Arrowcross to Netherton House.

'His name's Fritz,' Norah explained, attending expertly to Merlin. 'Snowball was lame when I walked him round the yard at seven this morning.'

'Firebomb Fritz,' said Robin, recalling a Second World War poster that warned of the danger of German incendiary bombs. He was already having trouble with 'the wretched beast' as he slid the stirrups down the leathers. 'He looks desperately strong, Dilpickle, and quite untouched by the Christmas spirit. Look here, I'll hang on to his cheekpiece and the off-side iron while you throw an elegant leg over the saddle.'

But Fritz didn't want that. Every time Dorothy managed to slot her left foot into the nearside stirrup, he moved away from her, slowly revolving within his own length, his shoes sliding on the shiny Macadam while Dorothy hopped ig-nominiously at his side.

'Hang on to the reins while I give you a leg-up,' cried Norah, breezily; and a second later Dorothy was sprawled like a frog on the horse's back with her arms round his neck. Hunting whip and bowler hit the ground and in the same moment Fritz threw his head up.

'Oh, Dilly, I've lost him!' Robin exclaimed, mortified. 'Silly me!' Then, in alarm: 'Hold hard, Dilly, he's away!'

And he was – cantering along the lane with a clatter that turned the heads of the numerous followers who were either unboxing along the grass verges or already mounted and chatting with friends on the wide lawns or in the cobbled yard of Netherton House. What they saw was an unknown rider, rapidly receding, whose feet sought flailing stirrups while her white-gloved hands feverishly gathered in what seemed to her to be mile after mile of reins.

'How extraordinary!' cried Nigel Tenbury, RN retired, from atop his chestnut mare. 'Is it a stunt of some sort?'

His wife, sour-faced and similarly mounted, looked but did not comment.

'I'm going to find Norah Blanchard,' she sneered. 'What time shall we say goodnight?'

'Three o'clock. Something like that.'

'I'll ask her to join us for drinks. Pity about old Max. We could have had a little bridge before dinner.'

Dorothy by now had checked and turned Fritz and was posting back to the horsebox. Her husband was at her side the moment she came to halt, handing up the articles she had dropped.

'Daffodil, are you sure you want to ride this monster? I don't like the resentment I see in his face and I fancy he plans further misdemeanours.'

'If he tries anything else, I shall thrash him.'

'That would only make him worse.'

They started walking towards the house, with Robin at Fritz's head, gently holding the slack reins at a point about six inches behind the bit.

'Norah didn't follow because she feared the sound of Merlin trotting up behind might have made Fritzy even more unsociable. She'll be gossiping with Flora Tenbury now, if I know Norah, so you'll have to scout round for her. Amanda's maid has gone down with Dutch elm disease, by the way, so I've volunteered to help dole out the stirrup cups.'

Still in the lane, they were briefly screened from view by a holly hedge. Dorothy slipped her left foot out of its stirrup, raised it and rammed the heel into Robin's right shoulder.

'Add that to your tittle-tattle,' she snapped, bitterly.

He recovered his balance, inhaling sharply through clenched teeth.

'At least it wasn't my elbow,' he gasped. 'I'd have had to bang the other one.'

The packed yard was buzzing with animated conversation. Once inside it, Robin passed the reins over Fritz's head and into his wife's hands.

'Say goodnight as soon as you start feeling tired, Dilly,' he said, looking up at her. 'Never mind any rot about losing face. This is a typical Boxing Day Field – too big by half – and you may find it too much for you. I'm off to the kitchen now, but I'll see you before you go.'

Yard, lawns and orchard were alike crowded with restless horses and serene riders, some of whom circulated in the manner of guests at a garden party, hailing now this friend and now that in voices alive with good humour. Everyone appeared to know everyone else and all seemed united in failing to notice the newcomer in their midst.

Except Amanda Berriman.

'You're Rob's wife, I think,' she began, with a smile in her quiet voice.

Dorothy turned gratefully to find a whimsical, mature woman, effortlessly in charge of a beautiful palomino. Her fitted jacket was fastened with the Hunt buttons and the Hunt colour was sewn to its collar, one patch to each side. She was, she explained, the Hunt Secretary, and please could she have Dorothy's cap money?

'Welcome to the West Property,' she went on. 'Norah's not around to introduce us, so please call me Amanda and here is our daughter, Diana, with a stirrup cup for you.'

Dorothy returned the happy smile of a girl of fifteen who had paused between Fritz and the palomino.

'Vintage port or hot lemonade?' Diana asked, cheerily. '*Ich habe den Zitronensprudel selbst gemacht.*'

'We have a German girl staying over Christmas,' Amanda said, 'so we're all trying to remember our German. Where is she, Di?'

37

'*Sie ist immer noch im Bett.*'

Amanda wasn't surprised. That's where the girl spent most of every morning.

'She's here to improve her English, but so far she's proving to be little more than a walking appetite, monosyllabic when not completely withdrawn,' Amanda remarked.

Dorothy chose lemonade from a silver tray laden with glasses – some full, others already drained – and Diana moved on; but not before saying how much she had enjoyed *Fun and Games at Walker's Croft*.

'Yes, I hear you're an authoress,' said Amanda, with admiration. 'I'm looking forward to dining out on the strength of actually having met one.'

'I don't know about an authoress. I write schoolgirl fiction for money. My ambition is and always has been to write classic novels, but at the moment there are not enough hours in the day for both. Or in the night, for that matter.'

'Hilary must be so proud of you, Dorothy. And Rob too, of course.'

'They haven't said much.'

In truth, her stepdaughter had said nothing beyond that one-line comment on the choice of title. On publication day, Dorothy had left a copy on Hilary's bedside table, but it lay there still, exactly where she had placed it, and she doubted if the girl had even opened it.

'The Blanchards aren't readers,' she concluded, dismissively. 'The hundreds of books at Arrowcross are only show. They were bought from a secondhand bookseller in Wall Town, irrespective of title or subject, and when they arrived in a van, Robin, who was a boy at the time, was given the task of rubbing out the prices. Max is my only fan within the family. He's quite tickled by it all. He thinks there was a Blanchard who wrote novels in Dickens's time.'

'Rob tells me your book is selling rather well.'

'So well that my agent is already talking about a third book. He wants me to throw my pencil away and try dictating to a secretary, and he left a message for me before leaving for Christmas in Italy to say he's found exactly the right woman – a Mrs Prince – and she'll telephone me early in the New Year.'

'Your agent sounds like a hard taskmaster, but perhaps the masterful male is the one who brings out the best in you. You must come to tea here one day, Dorothy, and autograph Diana's copy of *Fun and Games*. Meanwhile, have a pleasant outing with us and let's hope we see some sport.'

Alone again, with embarrassment gradually and relentlessly colouring her neck and cheeks, Dorothy feigned preoccupation with what was happening on the other side of the boundary wall.

Hounds had arrived in the lane and the Huntsman and Whipper-in, distinctive in white breeches and elderly red coats, were calling first Starlight and then Melody to order. Max had explained that foxhounds are counted in twos, and Dorothy had silently reached eleven and a half couple when Robin asked for her empty glass.

'How d'you feel, darling? I've been kept frightfully busy,' he said, glancing round anxiously. 'God, the Field's getting bigger and bigger! Aren't you just a teenzy-weenzy bit nervous?'

'Shut up!' Dorothy hissed. 'If you don't stop talking like a girl, I'll give you something to sing about when I get you home.'

Her husband looked up, shading his blue eyes against the pale yet intense sunlight. His shoulder was stiffening and beginning to throb.

'I'll go and help Di wash the pots,' he said. 'Sit deep, Dilly, and good luck.'

He turned away, then called back over his shoulder, 'I'll be following with the box.'

'Oak or elm?' murmured a rich, male voice immediately behind Dorothy.

A woman laughed delightedly.

Dorothy glared rigidly at the scene in the lane, where the Master of Foxhounds, astride a dappled grey, was calling for the followers' attention. Their conversation, boisterous now and shot through with shouts of laughter, slowly died down.

'Freddy Fox has been making a nuisance of himself down at Coomby's,' he announced, 'so our first draw will be Brooksmouth Covert between the river and the railway line. Stick together, but I don't want to see bunching at jumps, and if you must talk during the draw, for God's sake talk quietly. All right, then, we're off!'

Dorothy checked Fritz's girth, hitched it tighter by two holes and chided him aloud for blowing out. Then Norah came into view, albeit briefly, calling to her from twenty feet away, her voice coming loud and clear between several intervening riders.

'Send Fritz forward, Dorothy, before he pricks his hind quarters on Mrs Berriman's hollies and starts a stampede. Didn't you notice he was moving backwards?'

Ignoring her, Dorothy touched Fritz with her heels and they entered the general drift that was funnelling through the open gates and into Netherton Lane.

'Cracking day for the chase, don't you think?' began Nigel Tenbury, without introducing himself. He liked creamy brunettes, especially when they were smartly turned out and wearing a hairnet. 'I do appreciate these sharp mornings, when the bare trees are black against the grey mist. It makes me love England that extra bit more.'

The full Field was in rising trot, clattering along three abreast behind the Master, hounds having gone on ahead with the Hunt Servants.

'I was jolly glad to hear the trickle of the thaw as I went up to bed last night,' Dorothy piped in reply, carefully reproducing the accent and intonation of the people surrounding her. "Good!" I said to myself, "I can hunt tomorrow." My country is the Arrowcross, and we don't turn out if there's been three nights in a row of hard frost.'

'Same with the WP. My wife and I are members of both.'

'Weather like this usually makes for a good scent,' remarked Dorothy, borrowing again from the Blanchards' store of knowledge.

'More especially in the afternoons. Orf'n just when one is about to say goodnight. How d'you find Fritz?'

'Self-willed.'

'He loves his hunting. Just wait till the turf tickles his frogs. I know the chap Max bought him orf. Donald Menzies, nephew of Lennie Menzies, the racehorse trainer. Up in Yorkshire.'

The column swung off the lane and onto a grass-grown track, and Dorothy felt herself steadily pulled forward until she was directly behind the flicking tail of the Master's horse and fighting to keep Fritz from forging yet further ahead.

'WILL – YOU – SLOW – DOWN!' she grated, through clenched teeth.

They rattled through a farmyard like a cavalry squadron, scattering fur and feather to left and right, then onto a field of roots, where heavy going steadied the pace.

Amanda Berriman was briefly at her side.

'Keep out of the first flight, Dorothy,' she advised, quietly. 'There's a pecking order in the West Property just as there is in the Arrowcross.'

Dorothy nodded, too short of breath to reply, and was never more relieved than when the pace sank to walk.

A huddle of sheep, wedged in a right angle formed by the meeting of two hedgerows, their pretty feet kneading the poached earth, watched tremulously as the riders, towering over them, crowded through a gate into a meadow with more meadows beyond it.

'Three jumps and stop at the railway line,' called the Master. 'Follow me and keep nicely apart.'

Dorothy tried to delay Fritz, but he got under the bit and surged forward, petulantly wagging his head. As he cleared the jumps, with Dorothy seeming a part of him, a riderless horse with trailing reins came abreast then curved away on the near side.

Wild-eyed, Fritz thundered on, ignoring Dorothy's attempts to slow his speed. He was heading directly for the fenced railway line. With only a moment to spare, Dorothy used her right rein and right leg to put him on a circle that ended when she brought him gently to halt among the assembling Field.

'Jolly well done!' cried Nigel Tenbury.

Dorothy nodded, making much of Fritz.

'Jolly well done, yes – but are you aware that you cut the Master at the second jump?' Norah demanded, loudly. 'Go and apologise to him before he leads us to covertside. That's him over there, talking to Mrs Berriman, and you address him as Master.'

'Is it that serious?' Dorothy asked Tenbury, feigning uncon-
cerned amusement.

'It's not a case for powder and shot, but no harm done
just to say you're sorry,' he conceded, affably. 'Billy's a
good sort and he'll be glad to exchange a few words with
you.'

Amanda's smile was broad and reassuring as Dorothy
approached in walk. She looked perplexed, even disturbed,
when it became evident that Norah had not introduced
Dorothy to Sir William.

'What's this about old Max?' the latter cried, taking snuff off
the back of his hand. 'Down with the plague over Christmas?
Bad organisation, tell him. Had many a good day's sport
with Old Leather Bottom. We were young rascals together
in the Royal Arch Cavalry before they turned it into a tank
regiment and ruined the fun. First World War, of course. Ah,
well . . .'

He dismissed Dorothy's apology with the comment that he
hadn't noticed anything out of order.

'Truth is, I've had too much to drink,' he continued, with a
wink at Dorothy. 'By George, that was delicious port you
served, Amanda. In my book, port is one of life's compensa-
tions. I said to Minty only the other night that if there's a
happier combination than vintage port and stinking pheasant,
I'll eat my socks. Come on! Let's find Freddy before he kills
the rest of Coomby's chickens.'

Hounds were already drawing Brooksmouth Covert when
the followers, led by the Master, went forward in walk over a
stone bridge with the railway glinting beneath, then fanned
out in leisurely fashion over the pasture that separated the line
from the river.

Amanda stayed beside Dorothy, who asked her if her
daughter hunted.

'Di's too young. She's more than capable, but not old
enough for the WP.'

'We have boys and girls of her age in the Arrowcross.'

'Your country is easier than ours, as you'll discover this
afternoon, when we work our way over to Stanley Cottages,
where it gets quite banky.'

Dorothy swallowed. She said, 'Diana's very pretty and with

42

just the right name for the chase. Is she normally away at school, Amanda?'

'Yes. At Rose Choir. It's fewer than twenty miles from here, at Sweetwell, but she wanted to board so we let her. I suppose Norah's told you she taught music and French at Rose Choir before her marriage to Desmond Denise took her to France? Listen! Hounds are speaking. We're going to see some fun if – fox away!'

Amanda's sudden cry and pointing arm coincided with a series of short blasts from the Huntsman's horn. Then a fox – the first Dorothy had ever seen – shot into view, with hounds in noisy and tumultuous pursuit.

'Hold Fritz, Dorothy,' Amanda warned, with a degree of urgency. 'Let the pack get well ahead.'

'He's too strong for me,' Dorothy gasped.

She was nearly pulling his head off in a desperate struggle to keep from being carted.

'Sit deep, Dorothy. Deep, deep, deep!' Amanda urged. 'Begin to release him now that the others are moving. But slowly, dear. I can't think who turned him out without a martingale.'

Fritz started prancing, and for a moment Dorothy feared he was going to rear. Then he set off running, his nose in the air.

'Get your horse under control!' snarled an angry male voice somewhere in rear.

But how?

Breathless and with aching arms, Dorothy brought Fritz's head down by easing the pressure on the bit. At once, his pace flattened out into a thundering gallop that took him past the Master in a hail of turf and then straight over a tubular steel gate set in a hedge.

Dorothy came off while airborne, losing the reins.

She landed on marshy ground and got to her feet while the rest of the followers cleared the hedge and rode on. She had retrieved whip and bowler by the time Norah came back with Fritz alongside Merlin.

'Here! Take him and get back on,' Norah said, omitting the standard inquiry about broken bones.

Getting back into the saddle was like clambering onto a garden shed without a ladder.

'If the stupid animal would stand still for a moment, it might be a little easier,' Dorothy exclaimed, acidly, after another failed attempt.

'Well, stop digging your toe into his flank. You'd move away, wouldn't you, if I pushed my boot into your ribs?'

'He's too tall,' Dorothy snapped.

'Give him back to me and I'll hold him while you use that tree stump as a mounting block. Otherwise, we'll still be here at sunset.'

They presently moved off side by side.

'Stay in walk till Fritz calms down,' said Norah.

'Is that possible?'

'Well, it's you who's making him agitated, Dorothy, because you're agitated yourself and a rider's state of mind quickly transfers itself to a sensitive horse. Fritz isn't Snowball.'

'I've noticed.'

'Fritz has fire in his belly, and you must learn to master him, and indeed any horse, if you want to be welcome on the hunting field.'

They went into rising trot.

'The others are by Warren Station, so we cross the line here. There's a field of plough over the rise, then a hedge to jump and then a downhill stretch to covertside. Ask for canter now and keep it. Don't under any circumstances let Fritz gallop or you'll lose him again.'

Exhausted, Dorothy was haunted by the fear that she would leave the field on a stretcher. The clock on Netherton Parish Church told her that there remained at least two hours before she could say goodnight without admitting defeat, and her thoughts strayed to the wife of the dental surgeon for whom she had worked before turning her back on Liverpool. Brenda Fetlar had died a creeping death from gangrene resulting from a fall from a horse. A bay horse.

She kept Fritz in canter over the ploughed field and cleared the jump abreast of Norah on Merlin. She saw the rest of the Field a good quarter of a mile away at the bottom of a long sweep of wet grassland.

So did Fritz.

'Stop fighting him!' Norah shouted, impatiently.

'He wants to gallop,' Dorothy panted.

44

'Well, of course he wants to gallop, you simpleton. So does Merlin. But you must show him who's in charge. You're expert at bossing people around. Now let me see you boss Fritz.'

Dorothy was heaving on the reins, her bottom six inches out of the saddle. Then, as her strength gave out, Fritz leapt forward.

He pelted down the slope. Sitting deeper now and deliberately calming herself, Dorothy began sawing his mouth with the bit in the hope of slowing him.

But he pounded on, completely out of control, and some fifty riders watched, awestruck, as he bore down on them. Then, as they parted like the Red Sea, he entered their midst and stopped as abruptly as only horses can. Sliding head first down his forehand, Dorothy came to rest, still holding the reins, in the soft soil of a molehill.

'Still intact, m'dyar?' cried Nigel Tenbury, his horse's hooves whispering through the grass as he came up in trot. 'Not having much luck, are you?'

Norah arrived.

'Get back on, Dorothy,' she commanded. 'GET BACK ON! You do not give up on the hunting field!'

Flushed and on the verge of tears, Dorothy hauled herself into the saddle. She was aching all over, and her tiredness was so heavy, so pervasive, as to blot out further embarrassment.

Flora Tenbury joined them with the news that 'Freddy's gone to earth and the men are digging him out.'

Norah had guessed as much.

'I heard hounds barking as we came over the railway,' she replied. 'Have you met Rob's wife?'

It didn't matter that Flora stared Dorothy down through her steel rimmed spectacles, because Dorothy, checking Fritz's girth, behaved as if she didn't exist. Had she looked, she would have seen an austere woman in a black habit, the breeches of which were concealed at the front by an apron skirt reaching to the ankles. Flora rode side saddle and was never elsewhere than in the first flight.

'Not exactly a credit to us,' she observed, caustically. 'Or even to the humble Arrowcross for that matter.'

Dorothy was looking down, hitching her irons up one notch on each side.

'And yet she's just been made Leading File at the Creaking Saddles Riding Academy,' Norah told her friend, in a voice for all to hear.

A lot of riders were listening, although they appeared not to be, and some liked what they heard. None knew what a Leading File was, since none had seen the inside of a riding school. Like Norah and Hilary, the Tenburys and the Berrimans, they had been taught to ride – and to ride properly – by the family groom.

'You know Fritz has cast a shoe, don't you?' someone sneered.

Norah stared, crestfallen, in the direction indicated by the speaker's whip.

'Off-side hind,' proclaimed Nigel Tenbury, sounding brisk and in charge, but one step behind developments as usual.

Dorothy's relief was immense. It released so much muscular tension that she was at last sitting correctly.

'You'll have to take him home,' Norah conceded, a frowning scrutiny of the offending hoof betraying not only resentment but also a rapid mental search for some way of keeping him on the field. Then, in glum surrender: 'Jump down and lead him to the Master. Explain what's wrong and say goodnight. Rob will box him. That's the Land Rover over there, two fields away, in the car park of The Farmer's Arms.'

* * *

Dorothy slept all the way to Arrowcross, slumped against the passenger door, and she was still asleep, her high bust rising and falling inside her mud-encrusted jacket, when Robin switched off the engine in the stable yard.

He turned noiselessly in his seat, resting his forearm on the top of the steering wheel, and looked at her for a long time. At thirty-two, she was entering her prime. Studying her face, he saw not its hardness, as all women and some men did, but only its perfection. The small ears and snub nose, the unblemished teeth, the skin as smooth and firm as a rubber ball – these were as captivating to Robin as the half-closed fingers that reminded him of Pan pipes and the nails that were like tiny pink sea shells. He didn't lust after the body that was forbidden him, his sexual drive being minimal. He just longed to kiss her lips, her ears, her neck...

As if awakened by his gaze, Dorothy opened her eyes, then winced as she drew her legs in. There was grey mud everywhere – from her black butcher boots to the white stock that Max Blanchard had tied and pinned for her while she sat laughing and flirting with him on the edge of his bed.

'Dorothy,' Robin began, almost in a whisper. He loved her name. 'Dorothy. Dorothy, my sweetheart.'

She was staring directly in front, her grey eyes seeing nothing, her mouth a hairline of trapped hatred.

'Norah should never have put you on Fritz. He could have killed you,' Robin said, quietly. 'Father will play Rule Britannia with her when he finds out. If Snowball was lame, she should have put you on Merlin and taken Fritz herself.'

Dorothy came out of her reverie.

'Max isn't going to find out. Not if I can help it,' she said. 'We're leaving now. Go upstairs and pack our things, including Hilary's, and put the cases in the Morris. Be very quiet.'

'But Dill–eeeeee! We can't just take off. What about –'

'Shut up! I give the orders. Where's Hilary?'

'Round in isolation with Harry. They came in from exercise a few minutes –'

'Leave her to me. I'll tell Camilla to finish Harry and unbox Fritz. When the cases are in the car, go in to Max and if he's awake – but *only* if he's awake – tell him I've sprained my ankle, I'm in some pain, and you're taking me to Wall Town Hospital on our way back to town.'

'But –'

'Do as you're told,' Dorothy snapped. 'You're not to say I was on Fritz except in answer to a direct question from Max. D'you understand? If he's asleep, leave him asleep and tell Peggy we're going and why, but don't stay for questions. Hurry! I've no intention of being here when that poisonous dwarf returns. I never want to see her again!'

CHAPTER FIVE

Robin entered his wife's bedroom to find the wardrobe doors open, a pile of shoes on the carpet and a stack of dresses, blouses and tailored suits on the bed. On a nearby chair lay her hunting clothes, beautifully cleaned and pressed, topped by her curly-brimmed bowler. Her dubbined butcher boots stood beside them. It was the Monday before New Year, and Robin was still on holiday.

'Step this way, folks, for the January sale,' he chirped. 'Any bargains, Dillydown?'

'Mind your own business.'

'You're not leaving us?' Robin ventured, cautiously.

'You'll find out soon enough. See who's at the door. And tell Hilary to lower the volume of the gramophone before I take it away from her.'

'Yes, ma'am. Yes, Daffodil. And please don't go away. Promise?'

'Get out!'

Robin returned a few minutes later with the green-eyed girl whom Dorothy had met in Leon Grenze's office.

'Mrs Prince,' he announced, and left them smiling at each other.

'I wasn't expecting anyone till after New Year,' Dorothy said, 'and of course I had no idea it would be you. But please sit down, Mrs Prince. I've often thought about you, working for that ignorant little man in that dreadful office.'

The visitor continued smiling, her heavy eyelids half-closed, her head tilted backwards. She took a chair facing Dorothy's and crossed her legs. They were bare despite the coldness of the day. Mrs Prince possessed neither topcoat nor scarf, neither hat nor gloves. She had a pretty little umbrella, but that was at home in the East End.

Her Christian name was Ida.

'Sorry I'm late,' she said.

'Late for what?'

'For work. Mr Nolan said to get here for nine. It's twenty past.'

'Sounds as if there's been a misunderstanding, Ida. May I call you Ida? I didn't speak to Mr Nolan myself before he left for Venice, and he won't be back now till the third of January. My stepdaughter took his message. If I seem confused, it's because I didn't expect anyone to turn up for work. The way I heard it, a Mrs Prince was going to ring me up and arrange an interview to see if we could work together.'

'I can come back another time. Are you moving house?'

'What? Oh, no. No, it's not that. It's just ... Obviously, you can take shorthand, Ida, otherwise Mark wouldn't have sent you.'

'I'm better at shorthand than typing. Mr Grenze told me I had piano fingers, but he didn't mean it in a nice way. And that Miss Hoy – that secretary of his – said I had big, clumsy hands. I don't mind if you want to give me a test.'

Ida opened her handbag and took out a pad and pencil.

'It's I who need a test, Ida,' Dorothy said. 'I've never dictated before, except letters to patients and suppliers. The typing is less important, because you can work at your own pace. Excuse me.'

She opened the door and called her husband away from his housework.

'We're not to be disturbed,' she told him, sharply. 'D'you understand? Come in here and take my shoes and clothes and place them on the sitting room sofa. Neatly. A charity representative will call to collect them later this morning.'

Ida watched with a widening smile as Robin obeyed his wife.

'What about your six-guns and ten-gallon hat?' he asked, pausing with his arms full to nod at the riding clothes and boots.

'They stay where they are, because they were a present from your father and they'll fit Hilary before long, the way she's shooting up. Get back to your work.'

As a shorthand test, Dorothy had intended no more than a

couple of hundred words, but such was the totally unexpected release of creativity that the women worked on without a break until lunchtime. And while they worked, Dorothy's warmly appreciative gaze lingered ever longer on Ida's short red hair, the yellowish skin, the lowered eyes and the shapely and generous mouth that spread so readily and naturally into a smile.

Ida's erstwhile husband – dapper little Billy Prince – used to tell people in her presence that he had married her because she had plenty to get hold of, by which he meant her bosom, so ample and firm, and her meaty thighs and buttocks. 'I don't need no grab 'andles, if you follow,' he would add.

He had enjoyed her frequently – sometimes as often as three times in twenty-four hours. She dressed like a tart – always in short, tight skirts, flimsy blouses that revealed enticing underwear, a black velvet jacket and white court shoes that were scuffed and sweat-stained. She was careless, untidy and unpunctual; and these traits, combined with the uncertain health of her widowed mother, meant that she had never managed to keep a job for more than a matter of months.

When dictation finally stopped, a little before one o'clock, Dorothy remarked that she wasn't surprised that Ida was ready to leave Grenze. She herself had found him hateful.

'Oh, I've already left. He sacked me ages ago,' the girl said. 'Hasn't Mr Nolan told you the story?'

Dorothy smiled without opening her lips and shook her head.

'You tell me,' she said, softly.

'Mr Nolan rang the office the day after you came to see Mr Grenze and asked me for Mary Orchard's address.'

'So that's how he found me! The naughty boy. He wouldn't tell me, you know. He just gave his standard answer – "I have my contacts." Just wait till I see him! Go on.'

'I was alone and I didn't see nothing wrong with telling him. He said he was a publicity agent and a friend of Mr Grenze's. When he turned up with your contract the following Monday morning, I recognised his voice over the partition. I was typing and it was Miss Hoy who took him through to the back office.'

'I don't imagine Mr Grenze was overjoyed.'

'He nearly went mad. I've never seen anyone so angry in my life. He roared at Mr Nolan to get out, threatening him with the dogs, who were barking and snarling. Then, when Mr Nolan had gone, he burst into the general office, wanting to know who'd given him your address. I said I had. Miss Hoy claimed she'd told me on my first day never to tell nobody nothing, but she was lying to save her job. I lost mine there and then.'

'Poor Ida!'

Mark had been waiting at street level and had recognised her by her plentiful tears and the loud sniffs that accompanied them.

'He was sorry for what he done.'

'Yes. After he'd done it.'

'I wouldn't have stayed anyroad. Not with them two. Mr Nolan took me home in his car and promised to find me another job. Mam was ill, so I went on the dole – again! – and Mr Nolan brought me manuscripts to type and that helped us to get along. Don't say nothing to him, Mrs Orchard, because he's been very nice and he sent us a gorgeous big Christmas hamper from Fortnum and Mason.'

'I shall certainly say something to him,' Dorothy said, with a delighted smile. 'I shall thank him for sending Ida Prince to me. And stop calling me Mrs Orchard. I'm Dorothy, if you're going to work for me, as I hope you are, and my husband is Robin and my stepdaughter is Hilary.'

'I'd love to stay.'

'I'm going to make coffee and sandwiches for us. After lunch, you can transcribe our morning's work while I go through the proofs that were evidently stuck in the post over Christmas.'

Dorothy went again into the passage, this time calling Hilary to her. From the kitchen came the clatter of a knife and fork thrown down in exasperation, then Hilary appeared and advanced, her face stonily impassive.

'I want you to meet my secretary, Mrs Prince, Hilary. Show her to the bathroom and see it's clean and in order before she uses it. At four o'clock, come to my room and I'll have letters for you to take to the post. Off you go, there's a good girl.'

51

Hilary said not a word before moving off, Ida following. Back in her room, Dorothy crossed to her dressing table, where she picked up a list she had written out in pencil the night before.

It read:

Single first class Victoria–Gare du Nord.
Clothes to charity.
Pack selected books and all manuscripts.
Reserve single room Hotel Violet, Paris.
Tell Mark to cancel Mrs Prince.

Once again with a smile on her lips, Dorothy tore the list up and dropped the pieces into her waste basket.

* * *

Robin was ensconced in one of the easy chairs in the sitting room, completing his daily report to Sixen Toys, when Hilary came home from her music lesson, still wearing the brown pleated gymslip, brown stockings and shoes, yellow blouse and brown-and-gold striped tie of Holy Sepulchre.

'Shake your hat and your wet mac over the hearth, Hilarious,' he murmured, sucking the blunt end of his ball pen.

'Then hang them neatly in the cloaks cupboard and leave the door slightly ajar so that air can circulate and help dry them,' said Hilary, somewhere between resignation and amused contempt. 'How many times a day does she say "D'you understand?" as if we're all stupid? I just wish I could mimic her the way Ida does.'

Ida Prince had become one of the family. When Dorothy said, 'Funny! It's as if I've known her all my life,' she was speaking for her husband and stepdaughter as well.

'Where *is* Dotty?' Hilary asked, almost without moving her lips.

'Shh! Don't let her hear you call her Dotty, else that's what she'll go,' Robin cautioned. 'Ida is having a civilising effect on her and let's keep it that way. Dotty's in the bathroom, filing her teeth.'

He finished his writing and laid it aside as Hilary came over

52

to him. She sank down on his knee, slipping an arm round his neck and kissing his cheek.

'She can go dotty any day she likes, so far as I'm concerned, Bobbins, so long as they take her away,' she said into his ear. 'She was all smiles till she got you, then what a difference! "Do this, do that, and don't dare look at me like that." Candy saw through her and that's why Dotty won't hear her name mentioned. I thought she was going to live in France.'

'That seems to have died out, thank goodness. Strange as it may seem to a bollweevil like you, I still love my Daffodil. She's cold, I admit, but there are nice things to say about her too.'

'Such as?'

'She runs the household like clockwork.'

'Like a prison, you mean.'

'Our clothes are always clean and pressed and ready when we need them. She makes a dinner every evening that would make even the White Tower or the Acropolis look to their laurels.'

'I'd still rather have fish and chips with Candy and Derek, sitting on the floor, the four of us, eating them out of the paper. Oh, I know the flat was upside down and Candy could never find anything, but they were fun, Bobbins, they were human.'

'Listen! I want to tell you something. How would you like to go to Rose Choir School? As a boarder.'

'Rose Choir!'

'Shh! Wretched girl! It's a secret between you and me, and be warned – it may not happen. So not a word to anyone, not even Maud Barclay, and don't for heaven's sake bank on it. You know what she's like.'

Overjoyed, Hilary kissed her father again, then pressed her cheek to his.

'It would be wonderful, Bobbins! I'd miss you, because I love you so much, but I'd be home for holidays. Rose Choir! It's the best girls' school in the country. And I'd be with Maud.'

'And not ten miles from Arrowcross. But not a word, my little rodent. If Dilly even suspects you've found out, she'll drop the whole idea of sending you there. Now! Here comes

53

another secret plan. I know you miss Candy and Derek, so one day soon, but I don't know which, the two of us will have lunch with them. I drop in at their pub whenever I'm in Broseley and they always ask about you. We'll pick them up and we'll drive out to Kew or Hampton Court and make an afternoon of it. Shh! Get up! Her Majesty approaches.'

Dorothy came in, dressed for the street, and Hilary walked past her to the open door.

'You don't have to leave a room just because I enter it. I'm not a monster,' she told the girl, severely. 'And what are these wet things doing here? Hang them neatly in the cloaks cupboard and leave the door slightly ajar. Where are you going now?'

'I have homework to do for tomorrow.'

'Very well. Do that in your room. Go to sleep at nine o'clock and remember to switch your light off. These things cost money. Good night, Hilary. Sleep well.'

Hilary kissed her father.

'Say goodnight to Dorothy,' he said, quietly.

'Goodnight.'

The door closed.

'I sometimes wonder what she calls me behind my back,' Dorothy murmured.

'Our Lady of Great Homer Street. Don't say you're going out!'

'I'm going to Neasden to meet an illustrator. A cripple. She rang me, asking for work.'

'Neasden! Dilly going to Neasden. Such a journey merits an article in the *National Geographic Magazine*, if not a lecture tour. Why, it must be all of ten miles to Neasden. If you'll hang on for five minutes, I'll drive you there.'

'It's quicker by Tube. You need a rest from driving anyway. What do your new masters look like?'

'A bunch of gangsters. No, they seem all right. We had to assemble in the canteen and their chairman assured us nothing will change. Sixen Toys and Farr-Forrest will keep their separate identities. Time will tell. There's always a danger for the representatives in these mergers – a danger that one set will be paid off.'

Dorothy rested herself for a moment on the arm of the sofa

and asked her husband if he knew the Farr-Forrest representative in his area.

'Oh yes, I knew Tom when I was in the display department at Ketter's in Oxford Street.'

'Older than you?'

'About the same age. We have a dish of tea together at Lyons' whenever our paths cross.'

'Do both companies manufacture the same lines?'

'More or less. Farr-Forrest don't make soft toys, which is why they wanted to acquire Sixen. F-F's chairman called it "a merger for strength". Or did he say "a murder for strength"? You're thinking about something, aren't you, Dilly? Those little grey cells of yours are humming.'

'It's time I went. Don't wait up for me, Bobbins.'

'Bobbins! She called me Bobbins. I'll leave cocoa and a pork and stuffing sandwich if you're not back by my bedtime. I see you're wearing black nylons. Does *The Code of Pertinacity* say you can take liberties with your uniform?'

'Ketter's were out of cotton stockings.'

'Pray God they stay out. And new shoes! Bless my soul, Dilly! Black patent leather instead of lacklustre suede.'

'We all need a change now and then, Robin. Don't be frightened to come home, by the way, if you lose your job. Goodnight.'

* * *

Dorothy walked through light summer rain to the corner of Great Homer Street and Mortimer Street, where she hailed a taxi and gave the driver Ida's address.

She knew from Robin, who sometimes gave Ida a lift home, what to expect. Perseverance House, he said, was in a 'fight-a-night' neighbourhood. 'Umpteen dogs and kids. Pregnant women in curlers, puffing Woodies and gossiping. Just the place for Dilpickle.'

Dorothy paid the driver to wait for her, even if waiting meant an hour, and entered the stark and noisy complex.

Four tenement blocks were built around a courtyard containing a pram chassis on which unwashed infants were giving each other rides, while others played lustily in the gutted remains of a Triumph Renown. The lifts were out of order. On the brick walls, writ large in chalk or paint, were terse but pithy injunctions to quit the premises, deflower the Pope, and get the Tories out.

Dorothy climbed eight flights of concrete steps to the fourth and topmost floor. Monkey music, as she called Pop, blared from open windows as she walked with head up and eyes front past doors painted in nursery colours, most of them bruised or splintered or scratched by pets' claws.

Ida's was no exception. She opened it to a smirking, wriggling Dorothy, already babbling an apology for disturbing Ida when she was on holiday, then explaining that she had been to see an illustrator and was homeward bound when she noticed that her taxi was travelling along Rullerton Road.

'Rullerton Road! "Now who do I know who lives off Rullerton Road?" I said to myself. Then of course it came to me. Aunt Ida. Perseverance House. So I decided on the spur of the moment to drop in and perhaps meet your mother.'

Smiling, Ida led the way through a tiny cube of a hall into the lounge, flip-flapping along in backless slippers.

'Don't look at the state of the place. We're not like you, with everything lined up like soldiers and not a crumb of dust for miles around,' she said, in her slow, husky voice. 'Mam's gone very deaf, so sit here where she can read your lips. Telly's broke, so she'll be glad of a bit of company. She can't get out no more.'

'*Any* more.'

'Any more.'

Mam was slight and elfin, her legs so short that her slippered feet cleared the carpet as she continually swung them backwards and forwards. She radiated good humour, smiling and nodding even when there seemed little to smile and nod about.

'Can she get me a new 'ip?' she shouted at Ida, after the latter had introduced Dorothy as Mrs Blanchard. 'A new 'ip an' new ears. Dat's not ask'n much now, is ut?'

'Mam can't read or write, but she holds your books in her hands when I bring them home and marvels at them,' Ida explained.

'Am luck'n at a genie,' Mam told Dorothy, with a Dublin accent that residence in Oldham and then London had left unsullied. 'Juss tell me wun ting now. How d'ya tell a whole book to Ida in a pair o' months? Juss tell me dat woyle am still aloyve t' hear ut.'

'Stories pour out of her,' Ida shouted. 'I say STORIES JUST POUR OUT OF HER.'

'Well, dee must. Dee must.'

'Like bilgewater from the side of a ship,' Dorothy murmured.

Embarrassed at being Mary Orchard, she regarded with repugnance the characters and situations that entertained schoolgirls throughout Britain and even in translation. Her publisher was indeed Sandrew Morath, as Mark Nolan had said it would be, but her books did not appear under that most respected of imprints. Instead, they bore the colophon of a subsidiary called Marjorie d'Or Adventure Library. Reviewers had called her a latter-day Angela Brazil, praising the rich texture and narrative flow of her work, but it was to Cynthia Justin Bourn that she wanted ultimately to be compared.

'I'm like a Tin Pan Alley composer, churning out catchy little tunes when I ought to be writing symphonies.'

The lonely and difficult task of writing a quality novel in tandem with the school stories had been neglected and finally abandoned. But Dorothy was determined to resume it once she had completed a television adaptation of *Elsie's New School* and moved into the house that Mark had found for her in Willow Square.

'Does Robin know yet?' Ida asked, smiling and tilting her head back a little.

'About the house?'

'About everything.'

'No. You're the only one who knows what I have in mind. And you'll love the house, Ida, when you see it. Good square rooms, light and airy, and there's a mews garage, because I plan to buy a car and Rabbit will teach you to drive; then we can go off together to Dartmoor and see the old manor house where Cynthia wrote her novels about the Lampeter family.'

'The way you call him Rabbit!' Ida exclaimed, in lingering admiration. She addressed Mam, explaining loudly and with awe that Mrs Blanchard ordered her husband about.

'I cud see yiz doin' dat to Billy Prince, anna don't tink,'

declared Mam, still smiling and nodding and swinging her legs. 'T'was the divil in disgoyze was dat, if ever I seen um.'

'He was always making me cry. Used to hit me and push me into the furniture,' Ida remembered, bitterly. 'I was stupid to stand for it. He only came up to my chin. Sometimes, when he was going out after his tea, he'd pin me against the door and whip my face this way and that with his gloves. "'Ave a larss taste o' the ole rubberdubdubs," he'd say, in his horrible Cockney whine.'

Dapper little Billy – a plumber by day and a song-and-patter man in the evenings – was forever skitting at the way Ida spoke. To his simple mind, anyone who wasn't from 'dear ole L-a-a-ndon' was either from The Sticks or The Norf, the latter being a dark region whose inhabitants were still grunting round camp fires. 'Are yer frum Orldum?' he would say to Ida. 'Ee, it moost be reet gud in Orldum, specially in't Mumps.'

'He should have listened to himself,' Ida said, unhappily, to Dorothy, wishing afresh that she had dared return his mockery. 'He used the silly rhyming slang they have down here. "So wotcha dan wiv me dicky dirt, then? Coo! Tell ya wot, me dearest darlin': give me whistle 'n' flute annaver tickoo wiv the cloves brash, stedda jess st-a-a-ndin' there lookin' lawst".'

Dorothy seldom laughed. ('Dillyfower doesn't like anything that makes her laugh,' Robin used to say. 'Nothing upsets her quicker than a good laugh.') But she was laughing now, and watching Ida's face with admiring eyes.

'Your daughter's an inspired mimic, Mrs O'Grady,' she told Mam. 'It should have been she and not her husband who played the clubs. She imitates everyone, from our rent collector to my television producer. Well, I must be going.'

'I'll see you off the premises,' said Ida.

They paused in the boxlike hall, with the front door open and the inner door closed. It was twilight and the complex had fallen silent.

'I like your hair,' Ida said, huskily. 'It's still drawn back, but you've had it lacquered. And you're wearing a little make-up. It suits you. You should relax more.'

'It can only be your good influence, Ida. You've become my

58

talisman. Everything Mary Orchard has achieved is thanks to two people – you and Mark. Will you believe me when I say that I haven't been able to write a word – not one word – since you started your holiday? I'll see you on Monday. There's no need to mention this visit to Rabbit, by the way.'

They were facing each other in the moonlight. Ida's face was a yellow disc, the lips black, the eyes like fat spiders.

'I'll try to be on time,' she said, softly.

Dorothy stepped forward, took Ida gently by the upper arms and kissed her on the mouth – a soft, slow, loving kiss that the younger woman neither resisted nor returned.

'I'll see you on Monday,' Dorothy gasped, unaware that she was repeating herself.

She hurried away with lowered eyes, her heart pounding, her face hot with shame. Later, unable to sleep, she tossed and turned and cried into her pillow and murmured over and over, 'Oh, I love her, I love her, I love her.'

CHAPTER SIX

Number 38 Willow Square was a three-storey terrace house of ample dimensions. Area steps led down to a basement in which Robin, by now unemployed, did the washing and ironing. Wider steps led up from the pavement to a black front door, beyond which lay a hall paved with black and white tiles. The dining room opened off to the right, with the kitchen and cloakroom behind it. To the left was the drawing room, running the depth of the house, with rear windows offering a view of a walled garden.

There were two large bedrooms at the front of the house, one of which was Robin's, the other Dorothy's. Hilary's room was at the back, along with a combined bathroom and lavatory and a smaller bedroom used by Max Blanchard when business in town necessitated an overnight stay.

Above the bedrooms lay the attic, later to become known as the schoolroom. 'This is where I split my infinitives,' Dorothy liked to tell visiting media interviewers. It was a spacious rectangle, close-fitted with plain grey Wilton. At one end stood two identical desks, one for Ida and one for Dorothy. They were solid mahogany, their leather tops matching the green of the steel filing cabinet and tall stationery cupboard. The other end was the sitting area, its main features being a sofa, a low coffee table and two armchairs, one to each side of a gas fire. A wide window gave a view over the residents' garden to the access end of Willow Square.

Every morning from Monday to Friday, Dorothy waited at the window for the moment when Ida Prince entered the square from Oratory Road, her right arm swinging across her midriff, her body tilted slightly forward of the perpendicular as if pushing against a strong wind. She was always late, always sorry, always willing to make up the lost time by working on after five-thirty.

'I can't be angry with you,' Dorothy would sigh, after Ida had yielded to her kisses but to nothing more. 'You're so loyal, so lovely, so much my Ida.'

Cocoa followed on winter mornings, made by Dorothy in the small adjoining room that she had had fitted out as a kitchenette. The two women drank it sitting on the sofa in the warmth of the fire.

'Oh, that's lovely!' Ida breathed, sipping from a hot mug clasped in both hands.

Half dressed, half asleep, unfed and sometimes unwashed, Ida came to work on the Underground, using the journey from Dockside to Sloane Square to comb her short hair and make her face up.

'When you come to live here, Ida – are you listening? – you shall breakfast with me and I shan't let you off with less than a boiled egg and buttered toast, or else cornflakes with honey and fresh fruit. How is Mam?'

'I don't think she'll come out.'

Work began at nine-thirty. Dorothy sat sideways at her desk, dictating almost without pause, while Ida sat facing her, one leg over the other and a reporter's pad perched on her thigh. Her typing, which occupied her afternoons, was hit or miss, but she was unmatched as a stenographer. At eleven o'clock, they stopped for refreshment and conversation.

'How does Robin like being a housewife?' Ida asked, huskily, and with sly amusement.

To her, it seemed incredible, even contemptible, that a man could and would do what she regarded as woman's work.

'It keeps him out of mischief while he writes after jobs. He's not a man with hobbies or inner resources, which is why he can't bear to be alone. He used to go train spotting and he likes listening to dance music, but beyond that ... His weekends at Arrowcross, when I let him go, are a bit more adventurous. He helps Hilary and Camilla with the horses and there's the inevitable bridge after dinner.'

'Hilary has started writing to me, by the way.'

'You said. What does she write about? Apart from horses.'

'Mostly Rose Choir. She loves it. Does she never write to you?'

'She sends her regards in her weekly letter to Robin. That's quite sufficient. He tells me she's in the school orchestra and about to become editress of the school magazine.'

'He's so proud of her. Where did you first meet him? At Arrowcross?'

'No. I didn't know Arrowcross existed until Robin took me there to celebrate our engagement. He and Max had nothing to do with each other for several years; but Norah, being a woman, always kept in touch with Robin and she saw our engagement as a way of bringing father and son together again. She's not Robin's mother, of course, but she worried about his welfare and more so Hilary's, and she was very pleased when he married again.'

'His first wife was lovely. That's her portrait, isn't it, at Hilary's bedside?'

Dorothy nodded.

'Wendy Blanchard. She died when Hilary was seven.'

'She fell under a Tube train, didn't she?'

'Robin isn't sure. Did she fall or was it suicide? She was an alcoholic and very unstable. Robin never knew what state she'd be in when he came home from Ketter's or if she'd be there at all. I met him when he came to the surgery in Harley Street for a course of dental treatment, and we married in the following May.'

'Have you rued the day?'

'I haven't. I don't know if he has.'

'Were you in love with him?'

'No. I was twenty-nine, living in one room with a gas ring and crushed by the repeated rejection of a novel I'd taken so much time and trouble to write. Robin seemed to like me, and I wasn't frightened of him. He wasn't the standard male, coming home and slobbering over his woman. At the end of our first date, I knew I could do as I pleased with him.'

Ida was smiling.

'You beat him, don't you?'

'I what?'

'You beat him with a cane.'

'Don't be ridiculous! D'you think he'd stand for that?'

Ida got up, still with a knowing smile on her lips, and walked over to the stationery cupboard. Standing on tiptoe, she groped about on top of it until her fingers closed round the cane's handle.

'What's this for?' she asked, gently. She cut the air with it. 'You're blushing, Dilly. It's the first time I've seen you lost for words.'

'How did you find out?'

'I had my suspicions. Scolding him is only one step away from hitting him. Then one afternoon I came back for my umbrella. I'd left it in the kitchen. I let myself in with my key. You had Robin up here, in this room, and you were shouting at him. I felt like a criminal, standing listening in the hall, but I stayed long enough to hear you whacking him and him howling. As for the cane, its natural hiding place would be where children can't find it.'

'I don't want anyone else to know, Ida.'

'I won't say anything. What couples do in the privacy of their own homes is nobody's business but their own. But I'd love to see a demonstration. D'you ever have an open day?'

'Finish your coffee. It's time we got back to work. And put Exhibit "A" back where you found it, please.'

Dictation continued without a break until one o'clock, when Dorothy began putting things away and Ida went into the kitchenette to fill the percolator. At one-fifteen, Robin tapped on the door before entering. He placed a tray of sandwiches on the low table in front of the fire, then walked smartly towards Dorothy with a letter in his hand and a smile on his lips.

'News, Daffodil! Priceless news,' he announced, his pride visibly restored. 'Rabbit's got a job. The Pabay Linoleum Company. Central London representative. We'll have a car again. A swish Vauxhall Victor. I start on the first of the month. *Tenez, ma vieille!*'

His wife took the letter, tore it up and threw the scraps into the wastepaper bin.

'You're not going,' she told him, coldly. 'I want you here to keep house and run errands.'

'What!'

'You heard what I said, Robin. I've decided you're going to wear the skirt permanently.'

Robin stared in amazement at Dorothy, then at Ida, who was watching and listening appreciatively from the doorway of the kitchenette.

'Dorothy will spank you if you don't do as you're told,' Ida said, loudly. 'She'll put you over her knee, won't you, Dilly?'

'This is crazy! Robin exclaimed, all but choking on the words as his unbelieving eyes darted from one woman to the other. 'If you think I'm –'

Ida winced as Dorothy slapped his face, threw him against the wall and slapped him again.

'Don't dare raise your voice to me,' she shouted. 'Have you forgotten what I do to you when you're impertinent? Fetch the cane, Ida. You're going to see my husband beaten.'

Dorothy hit him again as he made to speak and told him he would get her knee in his groin if he attempted any resistance.

'You know your place. I've made you bend over often enough in this room. Go to the armchair. No, not that one. This one. And look sharp – unless you want both of us on to you. Do you, Robin?'

Ida was waiting with the cane. After passing it to Dorothy, she walked to the door and stood with her back to it, her big hands clasped over its handle.

'Make him beg for mercy,' she said, huskily.

'What a good idea! Hear that, Rabbit? Auntie wants to see you on your knees. Down you go, like a good little boy. You know better than to hesitate, don't you, Rabbit?'

Dorothy made him embrace her thighs, keeping him constantly under threat with the raised cane.

'You didn't answer me before, Robin. I don't like that. I asked if you wanted both of us on to you.'

'No.'

'Speak up. Your voice is so faint with fear I can hardly hear you.'

'No.'

'Better. Tearful, but audible. We'd take you down into your basement, wouldn't we, Ida? We'd knock you about in the old still-room, where there are no windows and the neighbours can't hear. It's something to keep in mind, Robin, if ever you feel inclined to rebel against scrubbing floors and making beds. Get up! Kneel on the seat of the armchair and bend over its back.'

Dorothy positioned him precisely to her liking before she began caning him.

'Six strokes,' she decreed, 'and consider yourself lucky Auntie's here, otherwise I'd make you take your jeans and underpants down. You will count the strokes aloud as they fall. If you miss one, I'll start the beating again from the beginning.'

Robin managed to keep the count, albeit hissing and gasping between cuts, until at last his wife sent him snivelling and clutching his buttocks to Ida Prince.

'You shouldn't be naughty,' Ida shouted in his face as he passed from the room with downcast eyes and trembling lower lip.

'Phew! I enjoyed that,' Dorothy said, bumping down, puffed, onto the sofa. 'Is this the coffee, my dear?'

Ida was pouring.

'I've never seen you look so happy,' she remarked. 'The exercise has brought the colour to your cheeks.'

'I do like having my foot on a man's neck,' Dorothy admitted, richly content. 'Especially when I can grind his face in the dirt.'

*　*　*

The day was hot, but the air cool in the dining room at Willow Square, thanks partly to a ceiling fan and partly to the soft breeze that lazily filled and lifted the net curtains at the tall, open windows. Luncheon consisted of iced soup, poached salmon with asparagus and new potatoes, sorbet and rice pudding. And since Max Blanchard and Mark Nolan were guests, Dorothy had earlier sent her husband to Harrods to buy a bottle of Chablis. Normally, she did not allow alcohol or tobacco in the house.

'Mary Orchard is not only the most successful of my Family of Writers, she's also the best cook,' said Mark, with a film of milk on his thick lips and a starched white napkin tucked into the collar of his silk shirt. 'My newest client is Lucy Reynolds, and lunch at Lucy's is always either bacon and eggs or fish and chips. But she's full of fun and a great admirer of your books, Dilly.'

'I haven't read hers, but she gets good notices and that usually means good sales,' Dorothy replied. 'Ruth Berrido had something to say about her on the BBC a few days ago. I think it was in the programme called *Books, Plays and Films*. I turned it off because I don't care much for Miss Berrido. I find her rather forward for a woman.'

'Ruth doesn't mince words, if that's what you mean,' chuckled Mark. 'Have you seen her on television, by the way? No, you won't have, because you've resisted the television invasion so far. She's an odd little woman – a chain-smoker, always in a black beret with a silver arrow brooch stuck into one side of it – but she's read everything and met everyone and what she has to say about books and writers is worth listening to. What did she say about Lucy?'

'I don't remember. Would anyone like more pudding? Max?'

'Television has in fact arrived and is in possession of the drawing room,' Robin told Mark. He looked across the table at his wife, who averted her gaze as he concluded significantly: 'Ida has won where others have failed. The monster awaits its aerial.'

'I didn't know you were Miss Reynolds's agent, Uncle Mark,' Hilary said. 'I'm preparing an article on her for the school magazine and she's been really helpful with information and a photograph. Isn't she young! Only twenty-four.'

'If you mention the bacon and eggs, I'll cut your tail off,' Mark warned, scooping up the last of his rice pudding.

'Would I do that, Uncle Mark? I'll just feature the fish and chips. Miss Reynolds writes for today's teenagers, the teenagers of the Swinging Sixties. Hers are the only books in the Rose Choir library for which there's always a waiting list.'

Dorothy placed her hand on Hilary's and said, quietly and kindly, but for all present to hear, 'Don't have too much to say, dear. You're not a grown-up yet, and some people may find your comments callow and even tiresome. And please straighten your tie. I know you resent wearing school uniform during the holidays, but it's only for today because I want

Uncle Mark to see how well it looks. You may change as soon as you reach Arrowcross. Uncle Mark and Aunt Sarah are thinking of sending Becky to Rose Choir.'

'If Uncle Mark can afford the fees,' said Mark, wiping his lips after interpreting a signal from Robin. 'If we send Becky, Rachel will want to follow.'

'May I leave the table, Bobbins?' Hilary asked. 'I want to say goodbye to Aunt Ida.'

'Ask if she wants anything to eat or drink, Hilary,' Dorothy said, while the girl, on her way to the stairs, was thanking her father for the meal. 'But you're not to wake her if she's asleep. D'you understand?'

'Is she ill?' Max asked.

'Just a tummy upset. We're going to Dartmoor for a few days while Robin and Hilary are with you and Norah at Arrowcross. Ida needs a rest and a change of scene after the sorrow of her mother's death and the upheaval of moving in with us.'

'Dilberry is going to inhale the heady incense that lingers still in Heelis House, once the home of Sylvia Justin Bourn,' Robin explained, with undisguised mockery. 'She has the present owner's permission to view the tabernacle in which Sylvia wrote her masterpieces.'

'Before my little man pokes fun at her, he should get her name right. It's Cynthia, not Sylvia,' Dorothy corrected. 'And if his reading extended to literature, instead of stopping short at *London Opinion* and *The Railway Magazine*, he would appreciate why she remains the only novelist to win the GEMA twice.'

'I read *A Lampeter Life*,' Robin answered, his tone making clear his antipathy to it. 'Son called his father Pater. Pater styled himself Captain MC. Sylvia Justa Bore was Henry James in flounces and a picture hat.'

'You're contemptible,' Dorothy told him.

Max divided the last of the Chablis between himself and Mark Nolan and asked nobody in particular what the GEMA was. Mark explained that it was the George Eliot Memorial Award.

'It goes once a year to the best novel by a woman writer,' he added. 'The prize is five hundred pounds, which isn't what it was fifty years ago, but the award carries a lot of prestige. Are you motoring to Dartmoor, Dilly?'

'Yes. With Ida at the helm. She passed her test first time.'

'Thanks largely to a short skirt and low-cut blouse,' said Robin.

'What make is your car, Dilly?' Max asked.

Dorothy shook her head.

'What make is my car, Mark?'

'Consul 375. Sky-blue convertible. It was a demonstration model, Max, so I picked it up for Dorothy at a keen price. Are you Rob's next pupil, Dilly?'

'I shall never learn to drive. It's unbecoming in a woman,' Dorothy responded. 'I won't wear trousers either, or smoke cigarettes.'

'My son drives and wears trousers. He'd smoke too if his wife would let him,' Max declared, with blistering disdain. 'He doesn't do a proper job any more. You know that, Mark, don't you? He'd rather go out shopping and keep the house clean with a feather duster. D'you wear rubber gloves and a pinny with flowers on it?'

Robin's eyes were downcast, his fair skin suffused by a violent blush. He muttered something about there being more shameful ways of passing one's time, but he didn't dare go as far as citing hunting and shooting.

'You were right about Farr-Forrest, Rob,' Mark announced, loudly, seeking to rescue Robin from further humiliation by a change of topic. 'Sixen Toys will cease to exist at the end of the month. There was a piece in the *Daily Telegraph* yesterday. The unions are furious, but what can they do except let off steam? So much for F-F's promises at the time of the merger.'

Max was still glaring in disgust at his delicate son, who seemed in his misery to be growing smaller, as though shrinking before the heat of a death ray. At last, after what seemed an eternity to his victim, Max relented, finished his wine and began to speak, with both hands flat on the table cloth.

'There's no such thing as a merger. There's only a winner and a loser; and the winner, despite the assurances he gives at the moment of take-over, will sooner or later obliterate the loser. The Sixen factory is for sale and I'm urging Blanchard Brothers to snap it up for additional warehouse space.'

Max was still a director, albeit non-executive, of the company that he and his brother, Simon, had bought from a distant relation named Etienne Blanchard on their return from the First World War. Both men had served in Flanders, Simon as an armourer, Max as a subaltern in the Royal Arch Cavalry.

'Neither of us had ever heard of Etienne Blanchard until I spotted a mention of him in a copy of the *Daily Herald* that someone had left in my railway compartment. There had been a break-in at Etienne's workshop in Cricklewood. The report amounted to no more than a dozen lines at the bottom of a page, but it made me get out at Stafford, cross to the opposite platform and return to London by the next train.

'This Etienne Blanchard, buried in a backstreet and turned seventy years of age, was making bespoke shotguns for the gentry. I telephoned Simon from Brown's Hotel and next day I met him with a taxi at Euston and we drove out to Cricklewood. We had inherited our father's business in Lancashire, but we wanted to sell it and put our money into something more interesting.

'Our search was over as soon as we met Etienne. He was deaf and working by gaslight with an old boy of similar vintage. Between them, they were making about twelve superb guns per year. Simon and I bribed him to retire with an over-generous price and he stayed on while we found our way round and recruited some likely lads.

'He was a craftsman, not a businessman. When clients asked him when they should come for a fitting or when their guns would be ready, he would look them in the eye and say, "I have no idea." I think he opened the post twice or three times a year at most, and once when the telephone rang he couldn't find it. He worked at his bench in a cloth cap, bib-and-brace overalls and gum boots, standing on duck-boards. We never saw him and the other craftsman speak to one another. Each had his own clients and they worked independently of each other.

'We changed the name from Blanchard's to Blanchard Brothers. While Simon saw to the technical side, I settled all the outstanding bills and gathered in the small fortune owed to the company. Then I bought a secondhand Minerva from

Archie Simons in Tottenham Court Road and took to the road.'

Before 1930, Blanchard Brothers had tripled the size of the Cricklewood factory and established their registered office and showroom in Albemarle Street.

'We kept the bespoke element separate from the ready-mades, of course, and a matched pair of Blanchard Supremes is as much prized today as in Etienne's time. At a duck shoot in Norfolk last season, I met a man whose father bequeathed him a pair of Supremes that we made for him in 1925. A man in your line, Mark. Duncan Macalister.'

'Editorial Director of Sandrew Morath,' stated Mark, smiling over his coffee at Dorothy. 'One arm.'

'I've heard of a one-armed bandit, but never a one-armed shooter,' said Robin, his aplomb by now restored.

'He's a lethal shot just the same. Needs a loader, obviously,' Max said. 'I'll invite him to Arrowcross when we start pheasant shooting in October.'

'Know Duncan well. A gentleman of the old school,' said Mark, his voice raised.

Truth to tell, he knew Macalister only by sight, having had him pointed out by Christina Foyle at one of her literary luncheons. Mark specialised in juvenile fiction – an activity that took him not to Sandrew Morath in College Square, Bloomsbury, but to humble Hammersmith, where Eddie Lombard held court as Managing Director of the subsidiary, Marjorie d'Or Adventure Library.

Max glanced at his watch, thanked Dorothy for an excellent luncheon, and said it was time they left for Arrowcross.

'Our cases are ready in the hall. I'll load them into your car, Father, if you'll give me the keys,' said Robin. 'It's priceless weather for a drive into the country and Arrowcross will be at its very best. Where's Hilarious?'

She was tiptoeing up behind him, a finger to her lips.

'Guess!' she cried, after covering his eyes with her hands. She kissed the top of his head. 'Auntie sends her love to you and to Panie Bracie and hopes we all have a super holiday.'

'How is Aunt Ida?' Dorothy asked. 'You were gone so long I thought you were playing chess.'

'I left her sitting up in bed reading *The Times*.'

'*The Times*, no less!' exclaimed Mark Nolan, laughing good-naturedly as he rose to his feet. 'That's a bit of a change, isn't it, from *Sweethearts* and *The Red Letter*?'

'Ida has embarked on a course of self-improvement. A wholly laudable enterprise,' Dorothy said, approvingly.

The party drifted out and down the steps into the hot sunshine.

* * *

A fondness for powerful cars was among the bonds that united Mark and Max, with whom Dorothy stood for a moment, admiring the latter's navy blue Lagonda while Robin and Hilary settled into their seats for the journey to Arrowcross. The hood was folded flat to reveal an interior of beige hide and polished walnut. Max was friendly with W. O. Bentley, whom he called The Tiger, and regarded the Lagonda's V12 engine as Bentley's masterpiece.

'Don't forget Saturday, Mark,' he said, easing himself in behind the wheel. 'You, Sarah and the girls. Sherry from twelve o'clock, cold luncheon on the terrace at one. Then we're off to the hunter trials with Arran and Blanch Clark, so it'll be a nice little party. And of course you're staying for dinner and cards.'

Dorothy, smiling at Mark's side with her arms folded beneath her bust and her high heels pressed together, was touched briefly by the jealousy that lay behind her occasional refusal to let Robin go to Arrowcross for a few treasured hours with Hilary. She resented the pleasure they would draw from each other's company, from the lovely old house of sunlit Cotswold stone, from its books and music, from its orchard and stables, from the fields and hills and glorious sunsets visible from its windows. Dorothy had loved the morning rides over grass-grown tracks, the long sweeping downhill gallops, the walks before dinner with bridge afterwards. To her dying day, she would covet the life of constructive leisure that Max and Norah lived at Arrowcross – he with his workshop and shooting, she with her gardening and puppy walking, both with their social calendar and winter hunting.

'Come with us, Dilly,' Max entreated, in a further attempt at persuasion. Then he added, wagging his head, 'Whatever it was between you and Norah is ancient history. And bring Ida. She can have Maud Barclay's bed in Hilary's room. We love a full house.'

'If you put Hilary and Ida together, Max, they'd be talking and laughing all night,' Dorothy said, side-stepping the entreaty.

She stole a glance at Hilary. The girl was looking at the floor, her face frozen by the hovering threat of her stepmother's company.

'No one ever died laughing, Dilly,' said Max. 'Now say you'll come. Say we can expect you tomorrow.'

'Our rooms are already booked in Moretonhampstead, Max. Another time.'

'Another time. That's what you always say, you scamp. Perhaps you'll come if I get Norah to ask you personally.'

'Take care on the road, Max, and all of you have a lovely holiday,' Dorothy said.

Robin and his father waved as the car moved off, and Hilary slewed round in the back seat to call to Mark.

'Goodbye, Uncle Mark, till Saturday. Tell Becky and Rachel –'
The rest of the sentence was lost as the Lagonda moved away.

'Tell Becky and Rachel what?' asked Mark, smiling at Dorothy; and, like all fond parents, relishing the chance to name and discuss his children.

Dorothy slipped her arm through his and they walked towards his car.

'Tell them to come to Rose Choir as soon as possible,' she suggested.

'Not a hope. We couldn't send one without the other.'

'Hilary looks nice in her uniform, don't you think?'

'Hilary looks nice in anything.'

'We had a blazing row over it. She said I was frightened of being outshone if I let her wear prettier clothes.'

'Nonsense! She'll need more than a pretty dress to outshine you, especially now you've emerged from purdah.'

'I've only replaced a black frock with a black suit.'

'Yes, but it's tailored to your curves and that's a white silk blouse you're wearing.'

'I've taken my hair up as well.'

'D'you think I haven't noticed? You're a woman in love, Dorothy. Tell me: have you never wanted a child of your own?'

'I miscarried as a result of the motor accident. It's as well I did, because I'm not a fit person for parenthood. Too self-centred. Too intolerant. Too strung-up all the time.'

'Too much a writer. That's what you're saying.'

'With me, dear Mark, writing has always come first. If this lovely house you found for me was on fire, my first concern wouldn't be Robin or Hilary or Ida. It would be the manuscript of my novel.'

'I hope I shall soon see it, and so does Eddie,' said Mark, thinking Dorothy was referring to her latest school story. 'It's nearly a year since he published *A New Girl at Walker's Croft* and you must get back to three or even four books a year if you're to keep your popularity lead over Lucy Reynolds.'

'I know, Mark, and it's so tiresome,' Dorothy responded, sorrowfully. 'I sometimes feel I'll run into the street screaming if I have to write one more word about gymslips and hockey sticks.'

'But that's what brought you to Willow Square, Dilly. Rob once showed me his salesmanship correspondence course and my eye stopped on one sentence. It said: "Keep asking yourself this question: what made me a success and am I still doing it?" I got Becky to paint it in Gothic on glazed card and now it's framed and hanging in my office at home.'

'I like Becky. I like all the Nolans. Is this your new car?'

'Like it?'

'It looks big enough to double as an open-air cinema.'

It was a Cadillac convertible, dazzling white in the afternoon sun. The electrically operated hood was lowered, exposing black twill upholstery and a cream steering wheel complete with sun-starred hornring. Some might have said it carried too much chromium, too many lights and an aerial too many, but Mark wouldn't have cared. Like his sumptuous home in Norris Green, his mink-wrapped wife and ballet-dancing daughters, it symbolised success – a success due in part (and he was the first to admit it) to Mary Orchard.

Radio Luxembourg sprang to life as he started the engine.

73

'There's Auntie!' he exclaimed, looking up and waving at Ida's bedroom. 'The face at the window.'

Dorothy turned, smiling, to wave at the lone figure standing back among billowing net. Ida was looking directly at her, but returning neither her smile nor her wave. The absence of expression in the moon face, more eloquent than any overt invitation, made Dorothy look away in confusion.

Mark was releasing the handbrake. He had a Gauloise tilted upwards in his negroid lips, his Zeiss sunglasses keeping its smoke out of his eyes.

'Thanks for a lovely lunch, Dilly. I'm hopeful we'll see you at Arrowcross before very long.'

'Maybe. Who knows? Goodbye, Mark.'

He waved again, sounded a double blast on his Windtone horns, and swished off in an impressive surge of power.

Dorothy turned again to Ida's window. The lone figure, still as a statue, had gone. She went into the house, closed the front door, and moved briskly from room to room, moving and tidying things that needed neither, until finally she faced the stairs and started to climb.

Ida's door was wide open. Ida stood facing her dressing table, naked except for a short navy slip, tilting scent onto the pad of one finger, then pressing it behind first one ear and then the other.

Dorothy hesitated at the threshold and their eyes met in the looking glass – Ida's sultry with contemptuous challenge, Dorothy's still troubled by uncertainty.

'Are you better?' she asked, nervously.

Ida went on looking and scenting herself, but did not answer.

Holding her breath, Dorothy walked across the room. Her heart was pounding. She slid her arms round Ida's waist, closed her eyes and began swaying.

'Oh, my darling, my darling, my darling Ida,' she breathed, all but crooning the words as she rubbed her cheek against Ida's and ran her hands over Ida's breasts, hips and stomach. 'I've waited so long...'

'Is the house locked?'

'Yes.'

74

'Back and front?'
'Yes. We're alone. For a whole fortnight.'
'Better get undressed then.'

CHAPTER SEVEN

'At least we know where she is for the rest of the evening,' said Robin, after lighting Ida's cigarette and then his own. 'She'd have a duck egg if she could see us puffing away and supping gin in her elegant drawing room.'

'We must be sure to hide everything and open the windows before she gets back. I'll see to the bottle. I'll tuck it away in a dark corner of my wardrobe.'

'Remember to wash your mouth out. Same as we do after our nights out.'

They were side by side on one of the three matched sofas, waiting for Dorothy to appear on the screen for another television interview. The black and white receiver that Ida had brought from Perseverance House had soon been replaced by a large-screen colour television encased in a mahogany cabinet with roller-shutter doors. Unobtrusively handsome, it harmonised with the mature furniture and antique prints that Dorothy and Ida had selected at house sales and auction rooms.

'Dotty's funny about equipment that other people have used,' Robin said, mindful of the distaste with which she had watched the arrival of Mam's cheap and none-too-clean receiver. 'Mind you, Dotty's funny about most things.'

'Dorothy is a genius,' Ida stated, clearly and firmly, as if explaining to one who would never be familiar with the subtleties of the human mind. 'She's not like other people. If she was, she wouldn't be a genius.'

Dorothy had become Ida's heroine. Dorothy was the imperious beauty who dominated her husband, the acclaimed authoress at ease with all classes, the aesthete who was teaching Ida French and guiding her reading. Ida copied Dorothy's accent and intonation, her gestures and habitual expressions, even her 'uniform'. The sheer blouses, the shell jackets (Robin called them bum-starvers) and slit skirts, the bare legs and those bruised once-white court shoes – these had gradually given way to black tailored suits, white blouses, black high-heeled shoes and dark nylons.

'Here's Dorothy now,' she said, nodding at the television screen. 'Put the light out.'

Ida sat forward and began absently scratching one knee.

'She looks nice, doesn't she?' she murmured. 'But who's the interviewer? It's supposed to be a man.'

'He's probably stuck in traffic somewhere. That's Ruth Berrido. She does a book page in one of the papers.'

'Oh, dearie me! Dotty doesn't like her. Look at her face.'

'It's probably Ruthy's cigarette.'

Ruth introduced Dorothy as Mary Orchard and followed a few biographical details with criticism of her latest book.

RUTH: You describe a party of senior gals attending a dance at a local boys' school in brown frocks and white gloves, although I've always understood that gloves are only worn with tiaras or when Royalty are present. No matter. Each gal draws a number in advance and likewise each boy – so Boy Number Four pals up with Gal Number Four and they stay together all evening. Are you sure that's what teenage gals want to read about nowadays?

DOROTHY: The book is selling quite well.

RUTH: But your popularity is declining, Miss Orchard, and has been for some time. I think it's because you're looking backwards at a way of life that you are sorry to see pass away. It may be a way of life that you yourself never experienced, but that you wish you had. You linger over it, savouring it like old port. You were born in Liverpool and you grew up there. What school did you attend?

DOROTHY: Swandella High School for Girls.

Robin cut in with: 'Liar! You left elementary school at fourteen and went to work in a cake shop.'

'Shut up!' cried Ida, savagely. 'You little toad.'

RUTH: Were you a boarder, Miss Orchard?

DOROTHY: No. Because we lived only walking distance away.

77

RUTH: I get the impression that much of your work is the fruit of imagination rather than experience and that Felicity Hatna's books have provided you with atmosphere and background. In your last book but one, for example, junior gals are allowed out only with senior gals and the seniors must fill in a card giving details of where they are going. This is pure Felicity, as were the brown frocks, but it was already out of date when she died and today not one of her Great Gable series is in print.

DOROTHY, without concern: Are you suggesting mine will shortly follow hers into oblivion?

RUTH: I think they might if you continue to repeat her mistakes. When Penny Bridge interviewed you last year for the *Merseyside Express*, she remarked on a growing tendency to teach and preach. She accused you of pontificating.

DOROTHY: I'd hardly call it that. I see it as part of my duty to uphold the Ten Commandments, to teach girls how to behave in polite society and to condemn slackness in all its forms.

RUTH: Wouldn't it be wiser to leave instruction to the schoolmistress and stick to entertaining? You have a daughter at boarding school. What does she think of your books? Let's say the last three. The earlier ones can stand up for themselves. They move quickly and they're full of sunshine.

DOROTHY: Hilary never reads fiction. When she isn't reading *The Field*, she's immersed in books on horse ailments and stable management. Her sights are set on becoming a Fellow of the British Horse Society. When she leaves Rose Choir, she'll go to an establishment near Kenilworth to learn yet more about horsemanship. I went with her grandfather to see this establishment recently and we lunched with the Riding Master, who is a friend of his. I shall use it for an episode in my next Mary Orchard.

RUTH: Have you considered setting it in a mixed school?

DOROTHY: A mixed school... No. I know nothing about boys except that they're rather disagreeable. Most of them remain so into manhood. While women are caring, catering, teaching and nursing, men are bombing, burning, raping and looting. I like men less and less as the years go by.

RUTH: It sounds as if you should write for adults rather than schoolgirls. Have you heard of Lucy Reynolds, Miss Orchard?

DOROTHY: We have the same agent. Mark Nolan. Aspiring writers sometimes send me their manuscripts for criticism and advice and I pass the best of them to Mr Nolan. Three or four young hopefuls have joined his Family of Writers thanks to my recommendation, and I wish I could say Miss Reynolds was one of them, but no.

RUTH: Her latest book, *Wandering Heart*, has sold forty thousand copies in three months. Why do you think she is so successful?

DOROTHY: I don't know, but I think you're going to tell me.

RUTH: It's because she writes for teenagers, whereas you write for adolescents. When you and I were in our teens, Miss Orchard, we were carbon copies of our mothers and very much under their control. We dressed like them, made up like them, danced like them, listened to the same bands and crooners, sat with our boyfriends in the same pubs. Television has changed all that. Television is more interesting, more amusing, more informative, more compelling than any mother or father – in a word, more influential. The one-eyed god rules, OK? Lucy is the first writer to mirror its liberating effect. Her characters – young people in co-ed schools and colleges – have their own separate and exclusive culture, with its own music, clothes, moral standards and entertainment venues. Aren't you frightened of losing your readership if you carry on writing about apple-pie beds and straw hats on the back shelf of daddy's cream Rolls-Royce?

DOROTHY, unruffled: I've already said I can't write about boys. In the same way, I can't write about jiving or rock-and-roll or little old children sitting in the twilight of coffee bars listening to jungle music. If the television teenager has left me behind, so be it. I can no more be Lucy Reynolds than I can be Agatha Christie or Barbara Cartland.

Ruth Berrido went on to ask about Dorothy's private life and was told that Robin had retired early from a management position. Both her parents had died before she moved to London. No, she hadn't any brothers or sisters.

'Another fib,' said Robin. 'This is typical Dilly. She tells lies if people stray too close to the truth.'

'Narry a word about l'il ole Idaho,' complained Ida, switching the set off when the interview ended. 'And not a hint about the novel she's writing.'

'I didn't know she was,' Robin answered, indifferently.

'She won't let nobody see it and I'm not supposed to tell anyone. All I know is that it's called *The Golden Gong* and it's all about a family called Sanderlin. She works on it in the schoolroom before breakfast and she's writing it in longhand.'

'Fascinating.'

They put out their cigarettes, moved into each other's arms and began the kissing that normally occurred only when they were out in the Consul together. Dorothy encouraged them to indulge their shared love of ballroom dancing, partly because she appreciated being alone in the house for a few hours, but also because she feared that Ida, if permanently confined, would become restless and go in search of new company. What Dorothy did not know (or so the conspirators believed) was that, instead of always going to The Orchid Room, they sometimes drove on to The Three Risings in Broseley to spend an evening with Candy and Derek Comfort.

'D'you think they mean what they say about buying their own pub?' Ida asked, between kisses. 'You know them better than me. Or should I say better than I?'

'I think they'll do it eventually. The baby has made them more ambitious.'

'Little Jamie! Oh, he's lovely!' Ida exclaimed, huskily.

'I expect they'll head for the Cotswolds or the West Country. Somewhere away from noise and fumes. What about you, Auntie? No children ever?'

'I'm too old.'

'Rubbish! You'll marry again one day.'

'I will not. Not after Billy Prince.'

'Give me another kiss.'

'No. You've had your ration.'

'Imitate Dilly. You know, it's amazing. You even manage to look like her. I don't know how mimics do that.'

'They think themselves into the skin of the person they're imitating. I'll try to do Ruth Berrido when Dilly comes back.'

80

'Oh, she'll love that, Ida. That'll be priceless. After supper.'

Ida got up with the comment that Dorothy would soon be on her way home and it was time the fumigation squad got busy.

She clapped her hands.

'Come on! Do as you're told, you naughty little boy. Unless you want me to spill the beans to Dotty.'

'If you spill my beans, you spill your own at the same time, my ageing Ferris Wheel. If ever Dotty found out about the man in the kitchen, she'd never speak to you again. I mean that.'

* * *

As a birthday treat, Dorothy took Ida to a West End theatre to see a turgid and short-lived stage adaptation of Cynthia Justin Bourn's novel *The Pride of the Lampeters*, with Clive Valance as Neville and old Faith Winkler as Elsie Lampeter. Afterwards, the two women went to the Ivy Restaurant for a delicious supper. Both wore Desmond Denise cocktail dresses and Simone Mirman hats, with appropriate stoles, evening bags and flimsy high-heeled shoes. Ida wore tulle over pink satin, Dorothy white crêpe embroidered with gold sequins. Such was their 'mess kit', as Robin called it, and it was aired with increasing frequency.

Always fearful of losing her, always deriving pleasure from pleasing her, Dorothy was catering ever more expensively for Ida's thirst for culture and her love of novelty and variety. Together they enjoyed the Aldeburgh Festival, Badminton, Glyndebourne, the Three Choirs Festival and many National Trust properties, particularly those in which writers had once lived and worked. On Saturday evenings, before or after the play or concert, they usually dined in the Grill Room at the Café Royal, where Dorothy told her acolyte about Max Beerbohm, Oscar Wilde, Conan Doyle and other men of letters who had long before cherished its glitter as much as its fare.

At their secluded table in the Ivy, following a brief look around to ascertain that they weren't being observed, Ida placed her hand on Dorothy's and smiled into her eyes.

'C'est aujourd'hui mon jour de naissance,' she began.

81

Dorothy shook her head.

'*C'est aujourd'hui votre anniversaire,*' she corrected.

They laughed.

'Well, whichever it is, I want us to have wine,' Ida said. 'Just this once. And please let me pay.'

'All right. But it *is* just this once. Not just the wine, I mean, but the fact that you're paying.'

Ida's salary, paid monthly like Robin's allowance, was high considering that she did not contribute to her board and lodging. When she attempted to pay for anything, Dorothy waved her away with the same words that Max Blanchard had used when rejecting Dorothy's offer of reimbursement after her long stay at Elmbridge. 'Keep your money for your old age, my dear.'

But Max was many times richer than Dorothy, albeit his wasn't old money, like Norah's, whose family owned half County Donegal. Although it bothered him less as he approached seventy, Max was still sensitive about being a first-generation gentleman whose wealth could be traced north to a chandlery shop. His father had been blunt Lancashire, though not as broad in everyday speech as he could be if he chose to baffle or amuse. 'If I was to speak right Lancashire, y'd 'ave t'ask ferra transilershun,' he would claim, perhaps before mounting his delivery bike and pedalling off, in brown shop coat and one cycle clip, with a galvanised bin or dolly tub perched in front of him. Outsize like his sons, he had an unusually large, hairless head and was known locally as The Tadpole.

Despite his efforts at concealment, Max's antecedents had reached the ears of his brother officers during the First World War and a certain captain among them had persisted in demanding, with arms akimbo and face thrust forward, 'Hast dun wi' pots 'n' pans fer gud, Walter?' That hated name had been dropped by the time its owner returned to civilian life, its last public appearance being in the register of the London church in which, backed by irreverent thespians unsuited to his taste, Max had married Pixie Tory.

'Pixie was Robin's mother, of course,' Dorothy told Ida. 'She began as a dancer with Emmy Reinhardt's Glitter Girls and toured all over Europe until she turned to acting during the

Great War. Her health was already declining when she married and it got steadily worse after she had Robin. Max bought Arrowcross for her and she died there of Parkinson's disease.'

'I get her mixed up with Robin's first wife – Hilary's mother,' Ida admitted.

'They were very different people. Wendy Blanchard, Hilary's mother, came from nothing and ended her life under a train at Leicester Square Underground station. She was in the Women's Land Army – otherwise known as the Cinderella Service – during the Second World War and she lived at Arrowcross, in the Nissen hut that is now Max's workshop, with seven other girls, all of them working for Arran and Blanch Clark and no doubt making much sport with Robin, who was tilling and reaping beside them. Norah had to feed them and provide laundry facilities and so on; but she was reimbursed of course by the Ministry of Food. Max had volunteered for military service early in 1940 and he was commissioned as a quartermaster. As soon as he returned, Robin left for London with Wendy and they were married in a register office.'

'Like me,' said Ida. 'But tell me about Pixie Tory. I like her name. It's a dancer's name.'

'Her father was a doctor, her mother a schoolmistress. Apart from that and what I've already told you, I don't know much about her. You must ask Rabbit to show you his album of photographs and press cuttings covering her theatrical career.'

'He obviously has her build and colouring. Blond hair, blue eyes, fair skin. You'd never think Max was his father.'

'Pixie was petite and very pretty in a fairy-like way. Ask to see the photo of her as Peter Pan. It's my favourite. She's standing with her right hand on the front of her hip and her left hand in her hair. There's an artistic streak in the Blanchard family that can be traced back on Max's side to Dickens's time and on Pixie's to an uncle who was a professional violinist and played under Beecham in the London Philharmonic Orchestra.'

Ida looked around at tables filling to capacity with actors and actresses seeking supper and conversation after their evening appearances. Then, smiling, she wondered aloud if

Hilary's talent for music making would develop into something more than a diversion.

Dorothy didn't think so.

'But you know more about her than I,' she continued, 'especially now that she's moved the last of her belongings to Arrowcross. Rabbit tells me she's just started work as a riding instructress.'

'BHSAI. She's got a job at a school near Andover, so she drives to and fro each day. A school in Exeter offered better money, but she'd have had to live in. How d'you like the wine?'

'It's quite heady. We need it to keep out the November chill.'

Smiling again, this time with an impish twinkle in her green eyes, Ida tilted her head backwards a little.

'You've lost your hold over Bobbins now that Hilary's left school,' she said.

'I don't think that's going to change anything. He still needs to be fed, watered, housed and clothed. He's under my foot until Max dies. Max despises him, but they're still father and son and Max isn't the man to leave his all to the cats' home. My hunch is that Robin'll get a pile of cash. Arrowcross will pass to Norah and later to Hilary.'

'Norah's a wealthy woman, isn't she?'

'Norah, my dear, is Irish aristocracy. Norah has cousins here, there and everywhere; and once a year they gather in force at one or other of their houses for several days of bridge and feasting. This year, it was at Norah's sister's estate at Settignano, near Florence. Next year, it could be Boston or Lausanne or anywhere else in the world where there's a little bit of shamrock and a great deal of money.'

A waiter came to the table and poured the last of the Mouton Cadet into their glasses. Dorothy asked him for the bill and Ida asked Dorothy if she were confident that Robin would leave her when Max died.

'Ask yourself,' Dorothy countered. 'D'you suppose he enjoys being bossed and beaten? He's on at me all the time to let him take a job.'

'Don't. I don't like housework.'

Dorothy lowered her voice to confess with furtive glee that

84

she had knocked him about the last time he 'started whining about going back to work.'

'You said you wouldn't do that anymore,' Ida protested, scolding her with look and voice. 'You promised me, Dorothy.'

'I'm afraid I weakened, Auntie. It was last Tuesday. You'd gone round to Maud Barclay's to return those LPs. I had him all to myself for half an hour.'

'Shh! Here's the waiter.'

* * *

'Does Bytheway House mean anything to you?' Ida asked, when they were back at Willow Square.

'Bytheway House. The name rings a distant bell.'

'A restaurant near Wall Town. You and Bobbins went there once with Max and Norah.'

'Oh, yes. What about it?'

'Hilary says Candy and Derek Comfort have bought it and they're going to close it for as long as it takes to completely renovate and refurnish it.'

'What do you want me to do? Reserve a table now for the grand reopening?'

'I just thought you'd like to know.'

The two women were undressing in Ida's bedroom, which had been Robin's until shortly after Mam's death. At that moment, Dorothy had moved him into the smallest of the four bedrooms, situated at the back of the house. Later, when Hilary removed to Arrowcross, he asked if he might have her room, which was bigger. Dorothy refused. It must be kept available for Max. 'He's a full-size man, whereas you're only a shrimp.' She referred to Robin's room as his cell and kept the only key to it in her skirt pocket.

'Have you never wondered what he does when he feels the urge?' Ida asked, snuggling up to Dorothy in the double bed that once she had shared with dapper little Billy Prince.

'I suppose he uses his imagination. Either that or he buys it. That's what he did before we married.'

'You mean he just picked up a tom in Soho?'

'Well, I don't think it was quite that crude. He used a girl called Stella, who entertained men in her home. Perhaps he still goes to her. Perhaps he's there now, when we think he's playing bridge at Arrowcross. Who cares?'

'What's your attitude to the Stellas of this world? The police call them toms. Billy Prince told me that.'

'I prefer not to discuss them.'

'I prefer not to discuss them,' Ida repeated, reproducing Dorothy's haughtiness.

'Perhaps you'd care to switch the lamp off.'

'Perhaps I'd care to switch the lamp off.'

'Just listen to that rain!' said Dorothy. 'How would you fancy being a tom on a night like this? Shivering in a doorway somewhere.'

'I wouldn't. Is it true they never kiss?'

'How on earth should I know?' Dorothy demanded, indignantly.

'Bobbins sometimes says "as priceless as a harlot's kiss". I just thought you might know, because writers store up bits and bats of information and you're forever making notes of how people look and what they say. I wasn't suggesting you'd ever been on the game.'

'I should hope you weren't,' Dorothy declared, with laughter in her voice. 'I don't think I like this conversation.'

The women were silent for several minutes, exploring mouths and bodies in the slow love-play that preceded penetration. During a pause for breath, Dorothy asked Ida if she would like to live in Paris.

'Never been. Why? What's wrong with here?'

'I just feel I'd like to start a new life after *The Golden Gong* is published. I'll be Dorothy Henderson then. Mary Orchard, with her scatty schoolgirls, will be dead and buried. I'm working on the last chapter now. Once that's behind me, we'll have a weekend in Paris and see what you think about settling there. We could stay at the hotel in rue Hamelin, where Proust died when it was an apartment block. It's near the Arc de Triomphe.'

'What'll become of Robin? *Où ira-t-il, ma chère?*'

'He can sleep on the Embankment.'

'He'd never survive on his own.'

'No, I don't think he would. It was only a thought about Paris. I wouldn't abandon him. But if ever he left of his own accord, this house would be too big for just thee and me.'

Dorothy feared that her relationship with Ida would attract unwelcome attention if they remained at Willow Square without Robin. The darting eyes of Penny Bridge, when she had interviewed Dorothy in the schoolroom with Ida looking on from behind her silent typewriter, had clearly detected something unusual between them. In the months since that interview for the *Merseyside Express*, media interest in Mary Orchard had declined; but Dorothy Henderson might soon become the focus of it and, in view of certain undertones in *The Golden Gong*, it could prove to be more intrusive and embarrassing. The solution was Paris, where *Madame Blanchard et Madame Prince, deux veuves anglaises vivant ensemble*, would go unremarked.

Before the lovers resumed their kissing and cuddling, Ida placed her finger against Dorothy's lips in a gesture of disapproval.

'You disappointed me before, Dilly, when you said what you'd done to Bobbins while I was round at Maud Barclay's.'

'You mean you're sorry you missed the show? I got his arm up his back and took him down to the still-room and really let him have it.'

'You promised me to cut out the sadism. Six of the best is one thing, but thumping and kicking...'

'I know. I know I'm cruel and I know I'm doing wrong; but every now and then I work myself into a state where I've just got to get my hands on him. I've had this craving ever since I was a girl at school. I used to hit my brother when my parents were out. Used to twist his arms and push his fingers back. I just had to see him cry and struggle to escape while I had him trapped. I'd be thinking about it and planning it on my way home from school. I think that's why I took so long to marry. I was searching subconsciously for the right man.'

Merely talking about her weakness increased Dorothy's sexual excitement. Her kisses became deep and prolonged and she squirmed about on top of her partner. Her imagination, fuelled by the alcohol to which she was a newcomer, was aflame with the memory of Robin wedged in a corner while she repeatedly slapped and punched him. He was helpless against her, knowing that if he fought back she would give him something worse. Experience had taught him to let her lust play itself out. Meanwhile, he just closed his eyes and kept repeating, 'Stop hitting me, Dorothy. Dorothy, please stop hitting me. I can't take any more, Dorothy. Please stop hitting me.'

'I don't care about his sufferings so long as I get my pleasure,' she admitted, breathless from kissing. She pressed her cheek to Ida's. 'But yes, I promised I'd stop, my dearest, and I shall. Just don't leave me alone with him. Next time you see me pacing up and down and twisting my fingers together, throw a bucket of water over me.'

'Why don't you put him over your knee and spank him?' Ida whispered. 'That's how some women manage to stop smoking.'

'By spanking their husbands?'

'By reducing and reducing until finally they stop.'

'It's too much messing round.'

'I'd love to see him face down, kicking his legs and squealing. Think how ridiculous he'd look!'

'I'll think about it.'

'Say you'll do it next time you feel the urge to knock him about.'

'All right. If it pleases you, my darling, anything's all right.'

CHAPTER EIGHT

W hile decorators were singing and whistling inside Bytheway House and carpenters were completing the riding school that Max was having built for Hilary in the field at the side of it, the Comforts were staying at the Station Hotel in Wall Town, from where it was only a ten minute drive to Arrowcross.

'Rob and I thought you might like to lunch with us, if only to give you a break from stodgy hotel food,' Norah explained.

'Tell the truth: you wanted to cuddle little Jamie,' said Robin, with a smile and a blink.

'Isn't he a rascal?' Norah countered, meaning Robin. 'I might tell you we're very grateful for your company. We've been talking to ourselves these last few days. Max is fishing in Scotland with the one-armed bandit, and Hilary and Maud are visiting l'Ecole du Cadre Noir in Saumur, thanks to Maud's father, who knows the director.'

She led the way out to the terrace for a luncheon of lettuce soup, spiced brisket of beef and cold caramel soufflé, with chilled dry sherry as an aperitif and Gevrey-Chambertin throughout the meal.

'Dorothy and Ida are in Devon, revisiting Cynthia's shrine, so it's only poor me and Robin who aren't on holiday,' she added.

The Comforts had matured since the old days at Great Homer Street. Candy no longer daubed at easel and wall, being too much involved in pleasing the public and nursing infant Jamie. As for Derek, all talk of 'the inescapable French-ness of – umph? – Mulsanne' had long since been subsumed by the cares of management. He still smoked St Bruno in a leather-clad pipe, and the languid drawl, enriched by time and alcohol, was now so well established as no longer to rank as an affectation. Candy had got him known as Dirk – a modification to which he had gradually acceded after resistance that was hearty but shallow of root.

On hearing of the Comforts' intention to buy and develop Bytheway House, Reklaw's Brewery had offered them the tenancy of The Tracing Board in Oratory Road, not five minutes' walk from number 38 Willow Square.

'Those who are mighty in word and deed have decided to gut the place and transform it into something a little less like the waiting room at Ellis Island,' Derek purred, with fluttering eyelids. 'Champagne and oyster bar. Gaming. All that rot.'

'But we wanted our own place,' Candy said, 'and we've just applied for planning approval for a bedroom extension.'

'Tell Panie Bracie if you meet any opposition,' Norah advised, roguishly. 'The Chief Planning Officer shoots here.'

Candy smiled.

'Where does this Panie Bracie come from?' she wondered aloud.

'It's a title used by the Polish nobility when addressing one another – a bit like "cousin" over here,' Robin said. 'Hilary picked it up from somewhere when she was four or five and at first we were all Panie Bracie. Are you confident you'll be able to fill your bedroom block?'

Candy replied that there was no competition worthy of the name, and looked at her husband for confirmation.

'We're casting greedy eyes on the well-to-do who come from hither and yon to visit daughters at Rose Choir,' elaborated the Broseley George Sanders. 'All the poor sods have got at present is that ghastly Station Hotel, where there's no parking, all-night shunting and a permanent smell of carpet dust and cabbage water.'

Candy was already recruiting waitresses and kitchen staff in preparation for the reopening of the restaurant. A little before the advertised date, she and Derek would host a dinner for Max, Norah, Hilary, Robin, various London friends and Arran and Blanch Clark, from whom they would be buying most of their produce.

'You won't omit Maud, will you?' Norah asked, moving to a wicker armchair now that luncheon was over and Mrs

Trapnell ready to serve coffee. 'She's part of the family now. Rob will give you her London address.'

'I'll check it with Ida and let you know,' Robin said. 'It's that white block of grossly expensive flats about a hundred yards from The Tracing Board. Ellery Mansions, I think it's called.'

'Maud's reading for a veterinary degree,' Norah explained, taking charge of little Jamie while Candy relaxed in the hot sun with one of her Gold Flake cigarettes. 'She's from quite a nice family, you know. Brigadier Barclay has just been appointed a Queen's Messenger.'

'They've given him a pushbike and an armband, but he can't use the bike out of business hours,' said Robin. Then: 'Hey! Just look at la Châtelaine nursing Jamie. We've lost her now.'

'Well, he *is* a darling,' Norah said, her smile marred by lipstick smears on her upper incisors. 'You can forget to take him home, Candy, if you like. Between us, Mrs Trapnell and I will thoroughly spoil him.'

'Nellie had a little cuddle of him while you and Derek were upstairs before lunch,' Robin told the Comforts. 'Add Ida to the list of women lining up to adopt him and you might be tempted to open a baby farm instead of a restaurant.'

'I do like Ida's voice over the telephone, although it makes my eyes water because she always sounds as if she has a heavy cold,' said Norah. 'It's a low, husky voice, which makes me think her zodiac sign is Scorpio. I hope I shall meet her one day.'

'She'd make an excellent hotel receptionist or possibly restaurant manageress,' Candy mused. 'She's not a bright woman, but she's steady and sincere and that's a wonderful smile of hers.'

'I'll tell you what: she'd make a jolly good cabaret artist with those impressions she does,' purred Derek, puffing away with pipe and flame until his lighter clicked shut. He returned it to one of the pockets of his scarlet waistcoat. 'She used to have us falling about when she came to Broseley.'

'I'm afraid she's changed somewhat since our last visit,' said Robin, regretfully. 'She has just the one impersonation nowadays and she keeps that up twenty-four hours a day, seven days a week.'

He meant Dorothy. In everything from preferences to opinions, Ida was now a faithful replica of her heroine. Lately, she had started making herself even more ridiculous by struggling to converse in French at dinner and by persevering with meticulous enunciation of English and scrupulous avoidance (not always successful) of northern vowel sounds. Levity being incompatible with her conception of ladylike behaviour, she eschewed laughter and seldom smiled. With her moon face, studiously kept immobile, and heavy-lidded eyes, she reminded Robin of one of those sleeping dolls.

'She's spoiling herself. I don't bother with the pair of them any more,' Robin went on. 'Sometimes I hardly see them for days on end. They're shut away in the schoolroom, speaking French or translating into French from Sylvia Justa Bore's interminable novels. Dilly's got Ida hooked on this woman and they discuss her between themselves as if they were writing the authorised biography.'

'Cynthia Justin Bourn! Good heavens, that's a name from the past!' Norah exclaimed.

'It should stay in the past,' said Robin, tightly.

'She was permitted reading for sixth form girls when I was a mistress at Rose Choir,' Norah recalled, tickled by the recollection. 'What a different world it was then! The only newspaper allowed on the premises was *The Times* and even that wasn't circulated. The headmistress marked certain items for reading aloud by the prefects after meals. Often they concerned India, where some of the girls' kinsfolk were among the Heaven Born.'

'Don't we wonder what the little blighters read under the bedclothes,' Derek drawled, sucking on his pipe with his eyes half closed. 'Was it *Exchange & Mart*, perhaps, or *Old Moore's Almanac*?'

'I understand it was *The Welder & Shotfirer*,' Robin said, adding: 'Did I ever tell you I was at school with the son of their drama critic?'

A cloud of red dust with a Willys Jeep at its epicentre was coming up the drive.

'This'll be the Huntsman, come to check on the puppies,' Norah said.

'Dirk and I will get going, Norah,' Candy announced, retrieving little Jamie. 'It's been wonderful, and thank you.'

'I'll walk to the car with you,' Robin said. 'Phew! It's mighty hot.'

They walked slowly round to the yard, where the Comforts' Vauxhall Cresta baked in the heat. Cocks, hens, and guinea fowl strutted about, while sparrows foraged among the cobbles and the two collies, Chappie and Ben, lay panting in the shade of the stable block.

'When d'you have in mind to give the dinner?' Robin asked. 'Weekend or weekday?'

'It'll be a Saturday, so's we don't all have to be up at cock's crow next morning,' Derek murmured, opening the car's four doors. 'We expect the London contingent will kip overnight at the Dust and Cabbage Hotel and motor back to town on Sunday.'

Candy asked if Jamie might see the horses while the interior of the car cooled a little.

'Step this way and meet Camilla. She's the groom,' said Robin. 'And a very pretty groom, I might add.'

They found her hanging haynets in the four stalls that were permanently used for the Blanchards' horses.

'The rest of the stalls will be got ready in the next fortnight or so for the first batch of school horses,' Robin explained. 'They'll be vetted here and given time to settle down after their journey, before Hilary and Camilla begin moving them on to the Bytheway Riding Centre.'

The party came back into the sunshine as the clock on the squat white tower atop the stable block roused itself with a whirring of cogs and clanked three times.

Robin cleared his throat.

'About the dinner,' he began, instinctively keeping his voice down. 'I'd like it kept from Her Majesty. As far as she knows, it's just another weekend at Arrowcross with my daughter.'

'Our lips are sealed,' said Derek.

'Don't even refer to it over the telephone. She's not above listening to calls on the schoolroom extension,' Robin confided.

'What a *monster* that woman is!' cried Candy, stopped in her tracks by outrage. 'We saw her on telly that time, didn't we,

Dirk? I could have scratched her eyes out. Narrow, selfish, opinionated, completely and utterly indifferent to everyone except herself. I can't understand what you see in her, Bobs. Never could.'

She walked to the car with Jamie on her hip, leaving the men to shake hands.

'Ask the man in the kitchen,' suggested Derek, with a broad and affectionate smile for his old friend. He gave Robin a soft punch in the chest and added, 'I think that's a little gem.'

* * *

A little gem was not how Mark Nolan would have described Mary Orchard's latest offering. With more than half her books out of print, her sales continued to diminish, as did her reputation at the offices of Marjorie d'Or Adventure Library in Hammersmith.

'I've come straight here from a meeting with Eddie Lombard, Dorothy,' he began, his use of her full name endorsing the concern in his voice and manner. He drew the manuscript of *Connie's First Term* out of his Morocco briefcase and let it fall on the coffee table in the schoolroom. 'I didn't think I'd ever have to say that Eddie had rejected your work, but I'm afraid, Dilly, that that's what he's done. I'll be brutally frank with you. He says you've thrown the words at the paper.'

'Sit down on the sofa, Mark, and have your coffee,' Dorothy said.

She sipped hers. Ida left her desk and walked towards them, seating herself noiselessly in the easy chair facing Dorothy's. Of late, she had started greeting Mark with only a nod and then working in silence throughout his visit. This morning, she had ignored his arrival completely and was now maintaining an attitude of impassive superiority.

'Did you notice, Dilly, that Eddie had rewritten a good ten per cent of your last book?' Mark persisted. 'It was that bad.'

'What right has Mr Lombard to alter Mrs Blanchard's work?' Ida inquired, coldly. 'She's the writer. He's only a publisher.'

Mark looked at Dorothy, having had about as much as he

could take of the new Ida, and saw the slight movement of the head that told Ida to keep out of it. She rose with infinite dignity and returned to her desk.

'I'm sorry, Mark, very sorry ... I'm letting you down and that's something you've never done to me,' Dorothy said. 'But you do have Lucy Reynolds in your Family of Writers and I think I've found you another money maker. He's a policeman; but no ordinary policeman, as you'll quickly discover.'

'I think you're preparing me for the end of Mary Orchard, aren't you, Dilly?'

'Sort of. I'll be more explicit next time, Mark. Give me a couple of weeks to rewrite *Connie*, and today I'll write to Mr Lombard to apologise for offering substandard work. I repeat, I have no right to let people down. If Mary Orchard is to retire, she must do so honourably; and that means with all her obligations fulfilled.'

'All right, Dilly.'

'How are Sarah and the girls?'

'Fine. They send their love.'

'Have a nice, relaxing holiday, Mark, and we'll see you when you get back.'

They rose. For once, Mark was without a smile. At the schoolroom door, Dorothy handed him two manuscripts.

'This is the one from the policeman. I said I'd found him, but of course I meant he'd found me,' she explained. 'This other one, *The Golden Gong*, is by someone called Ivy Robinson. A Liverpool woman, which explains perhaps why she sent it to me. I don't normally receive mature fiction, any more than you do, and I was on the point of returning it until I started to read. It's not bad.'

'I'll look them over, Dilly.'

'You're sighing. You're annoyed with me, aren't you, dear?'

Dorothy laid a hand on Mark's arm and his grin broke through at last, crinkling the fat about his eyes.

'Lissern! Dress *Connie* up in her Sunday best and all will be forgiven,' he declared, in a loud voice.

He said goodbye, ignoring Ida Prince, and found his own way out, calling farewell to Robin before closing the front door with a slam that nearly brought the house down. Robin had once said that Mark always did that, adding, 'Perhaps it's an old Ashkenazi custom.'

Tense and unhappy, Dorothy stood watching Ida, who was now typing correspondence, her face expressionless. She had taken recently to paint and powder, making up each morning from a box of theatrical cosmetics.

'What has Mark done to you?' Dorothy began, grimly determined to put an end to an unpleasant situation.

Ida continued typing.

'I don't like the way saliva collects at the corners of his mouth,' she replied.

'Is that a valid reason for turning against him? Mark Nolan is much more than a business associate, Ida, in case you haven't noticed; and even if he were only that, it would be no excuse for embarrassing him.'

'He's not what I call a Real Person. The richer he gets, the more his vulgarity shows through. Those gold fillings, and now fancy waistcoats. He should wear a plain cummerbund, like Mr Blanchard senior.'

Real People had been Dorothy's term for men and women of consequence, until further thought had persuaded her to divide British society into the Privileged Class, the Creative Class and the Unfortunate Class. Ida's appropriation of it was enough to ignite the anger that Dorothy had been accumulating for some time.

'I don't know what you mean by a Real Person and I don't think you do either,' she snapped. 'What I do know is that no one under my roof is going to treat Mark Nolan like a leper. So cut it out before we fall out, and don't ever interfere in matters that don't concern you.'

Ida finished typing and placed the letter on a pile awaiting signature, coming to her feet in the same movement.

'And for heaven's sake, come down off your high horse,' Dorothy shouted, as Ida walked loftily past her to the door. 'I've done everything I can to help and please you; and now, for some reason, you've started treating me like dirt. Well, I've had as much of it as I'm prepared to take. If you've decided that I'm no longer good enough for you, clear out!'

* * *

Ida failed to appear for sandwiches and coffee at one o'clock, and Robin said she was in her bedroom and wanted nothing to eat or drink. Afterwards, alone in the schoolroom, Dorothy attempted the revision of *Connie's First Term*. But after an hour or more of crossing out everything she wrote, she threw down her pencil in disgust and walked over to the wide dormer window that would have delighted a painter or sculptor. At the opposite end of Willow Square, beyond the residents' garden that was its centrepiece, black taxis and scarlet buses flicked past on Oratory Road. But all Dorothy could see was a painted mask of haughty indifference.

She turned listlessly to Ida's desk, in a mess as always, and tidied round until she stopped at the book in which Ida did her French exercises. Dorothy glanced at the last offering, peppered with corrections in her own neat hand, then wandered back to the window.

'Everything she knows, everything she's got, is thanks to me,' she thought, dismally. 'Without me, she'd still be chewing gum and wiping her mouth with the back of her hand.'

At half past three, humbled by misery, she went down one floor and tapped on Ida's door.

'Are you there?' she called.

'Come in.'

The double bed in which they no longer frolicked was piled with clothes and Ida was adding further garments from her wardrobe.

'Where are you going?' Dorothy gasped, frowning as she advanced.

'I'm not going anywhere. I'm doing what you were doing the day I started work for you at Great Homer Street – gathering clothes together to give to charity. Clothes I don't wear any more.'

Dorothy sighed with relief.

'My heart stopped for a moment,' she confessed. 'I'm sorry about before. I didn't mean it about clearing out. It's just that you've been so cool with me lately and I don't know what I've done.'

Ida allowed her cheek to be kissed, but turned away as Dorothy slipped an arm round her waist and went to kiss her lips.

'I'm a little tired, that's all,' she said, huskily. 'You know what it's like sometimes.'

'You've eaten nothing since breakfast. I'll have tea served in here,' Dorothy decided.

She found her husband in his room, which faced her own across the landing. His door was open. Following the conviction (slow to dawn) that he did indeed use his imagination rather than seek another Stella, she had forbidden him to close it completely at any time.

'What are you doing?' she snapped, standing over him with clenched fists.

'Packing.'

'Well, stop packing and go to your kitchen and fetch tea and cake to Miss Ida's room. Now.'

'Miss Ida, forsooth! Auntie has become Miss Ida. Does this complete the new image? Does it mean that the last trace of Perseverance House has been swept under the carpet?'

'Get downstairs before I lose my temper,' Dorothy shouted.

'OK, OK, OK … No need to summon the cavalry, Dillyflower. You'll have your tea and biscuits on time, just as you've always done.'

'Don't be flippant with me, Robin. I don't like it,' Dorothy called after him. 'Perhaps it's time I reminded you of your place in this household.'

Her manner softening, she went back to Ida, who was still sorting garments on the bed, and this time succeeded in encircling her waist.

'I'm going to punish him,' she confided.

Ida had overheard the remark about Perseverance House. Her reply was conclusive.

'Cane him,' she said. 'But no sadism.'

'Whatever pleases you, my dearest.'

They kissed.

'He's coming back,' Ida murmured.

Dorothy moved quickly to the dressing table. Mindful only of the pleasure that awaited her, she forgot she was in Ida's room and started applying Ida's face powder.

'Dillydown and Idadown. My favourite couple,' cried Robin, elated by the prospect of the weekend to come. 'Tea for two and two for tea. Where d'you want it?'

Ida told him to put the tray on her bedside table. Then, curtly: 'Just a moment. You haven't been told you can go yet. Dorothy has something to say to you.'

'Don't you mean Miss Dorothy?' Robin countered, with a smile and a blink. 'She'll have me calling the cat Mr Tabby next. Please may I have my allowance, Miss Dilly?'

'I've no cash, Robin, till Monday, and neither has Ida,' his wife answered, sweetly. 'Why d'you need it now? Is there enough petrol in the car, Ida?'

'Enough to get him to Arrowcross and back.'

'There you are, Robin. You don't need any money.'

'I may want to take Hilary and Maud for lunch or dinner somewhere.'

'I see. And where would that somewhere be, Robin? It wouldn't be Bytheway House, would it?' Dorothy ventured.

She was watching her husband's face reflected in the looking-glass, relishing his sudden alarm and noting the accusatory look he threw at Ida.

'No, Rabbit. Auntie didn't tell me anything except what Hilary told her in her letters. Shall we say I just put two and two together?'

'Confirmed, no doubt, by another of your telephone calls,' Robin suggested, with bitter contempt.

'Another, dear? I only needed one. I rang Bytheway House this morning and said I'd heard it was reopening tomorrow, Saturday, and could I book a table for two. The girl replied that there was a party for family and friends over the weekend, but I could book any day from Monday onwards.'

'Very smart. Like the two telephone calls you made from Elmbridge to Great Homer Street to see if your hunch was right that I had Candy and Derek staying in the flat. Hilary answered your first call and you hung up without saying anything. Candy answered your second attempt and once again you hung up without speaking. You didn't need to call a third time.'

'It's you who's the smart one, Robin, not me,' Dorothy said. She had turned to look directly at him. 'Fancy your remembering in such detail after so long a time!'

'You pretended not to know they were staying with me. You wanted the pleasure of kicking them out. So you signed yourself out of Elmbridge three days before you were due to leave and against Doctor Goldie's advice. He told me that when I went down to collect your books and typewriter.'

'Yes. You kept very quiet about The Tramps being at the flat, didn't you, Robin?' Dorothy said, softly, walking towards him. 'Not a word from you or Hilary when you came to visit me. And if I hadn't telephoned Bytheway House this morning, I'd have gone to bed tonight believing you were having just another weekend at Arrowcross, which is what you wanted me to believe.'

She heard the hiss of Ida catching her breath as she slapped her husband's face.

'I don't like deceit,' she shouted.

'Even your own?' he wavered.

Dorothy hit him again, even harder.

'You miserable little worm. Look at yourself! Weeping. Trembling. Terrified of what your wife might do to you. Well, I'll come straight to the point, Rabbit. You're not going to Arrowcross. Now get to your room this minute.'

'I want to see my daughter and –'

'Shut up! Don't you dare argue with me,' Dorothy shouted; and, Ida or no Ida, she slapped Robin again.

He raised his hand to ward off more blows. Dorothy grabbed his wrist, swung him round until his arm was up his back, then hustled him to his room, thrusting him inside.

She stood watching him from the threshold, her fists on her hips, her grey eyes as cold as a knife blade.

'This evening you're going to telephone Max,' she said. 'He already despises you, but wait till you tell him your wife won't let you go to the party. She's keeping you in and making you scrub floors as a punishment for deception.'

'He won't. Because I won't say it,' Robin mumbled, feebly.

'Oh, yes you will. I'll make you. I'll stand next to you and if you don't say it, I'll take the receiver out of your hand and say it for you. And I wouldn't like to be you afterwards.'

Dorothy closed the door slowly, backing out so that she could watch her husband's face till the last moment, then locked him inside with the key from her skirt pocket.

'It's time I took the letters round to the post,' Ida said, coming out of her bedroom. 'I'll fetch them from upstairs.'

'We'll dine in the Savoy Grill tonight, Ida, and leave Rabbit to starve in his cell till morning,' Dorothy announced.

She followed Ida up to the schoolroom and stayed there after Ida had gone downstairs and slammed the front door. Then she fell to pacing to and fro, her bust heaving while she closed and unclosed her fists. A pulse was bumping in her temple. She had about ten minutes if she started at once. Her plan was to burst into his room, pause for a moment to savour his terror, then say quietly: 'Now you'll get it.' Trapping him in a corner, she would pummel the wind out of him, ram her knee into his groin to double him up, then slap his face and keep on slapping till he sank to the floor.

But time was short. Taking three stout elastic bands from her desk, she hurried down to Ida's room and rooted among the garments on the bed until she found a leather miniskirt. Once her victim was on the floor, she told herself, she would kick him till he was yelling and could take no more.

Resting it on a hard surface, Dorothy rolled the miniskirt into a soft truncheon and applied the rubber bands to secure it in three places. Her fingers were trembling, her heart thudding. After the kicking, she would heave him onto his bed, put her knee on his chest and her hands round his throat and make as if to strangle him.

'Not a peep out of you. D'you understand?' she would say, pressing his windpipe. 'Not so much as a whimper until I come to unlock you in the morning. Otherwise, I'll give you some more of it.'

She walked briskly across the landing to his door, rattled the key in the lock to rouse his fear, then kicked the door open and went inside. He wasn't there.

CHAPTER NINE

After dinner on Sunday, the two women spent the evening at either side of the drawing room fire, where Dorothy finished reading Saturday's *Times* and Ida continued her ponderous progress through Pettifer's monumental biography of Cynthia Justin Bourn.

'She's struggled through every novel in the Lampeter series and I'll bet she can't remember a single sentence,' Robin had recently remarked to Mark Nolan. 'And don't think you're the only one who's fed up with her airs and graces. Dilly is too, but Dilly got her this way. Have you seen the reading glasses, by the way? She looks like something from outer space.'

The spectacles were round and unusually large, the frames matching Ida's luminous pink lipstick. With Pettifer Volume 2 held at eye level, she sat upright in her armchair in imitation of Elsie Lampeter, her knees and ankles pressed together with a feline primness worthy of the former heroine who sat facing her.

Dorothy asked what she thought of Pettifer's masterpiece.

Ida paused.

'It's a serious biographical study,' she conceded at last, repeating verbatim what Dorothy had said when commending it to her. 'There is biography and there is the life story. The two are not necessarily the same.'

She spoke slowly, deliberately, and with a measure of condescension, as though explaining to someone who might have difficulty in keeping up. At the same time, she indulged a newly acquired trick of gazing tolerantly at her auditor while moving her head slightly from side to side.

'Where are you up to?' Dorothy asked, her indulgent smile and warmth of voice aimed at unfreezing her companion.

Ida had resumed her reading. For a moment, it seemed she intended ignoring the question. Then, patiently: 'I'm up to where Cynthia has been awarded the GEMA for *The House of Lampeter.*'

'You're up to 1929,' said Dorothy, settling contentedly to the subject. 'By then, her novels went automatically into the library of every British Embassy in the world. It must have been marvellous for her. Her obituary notice in *The Times* referred to her work as "redolent of the Pax Britannica". By 1929, of course, she was at the height of her powers and a friend of Edith Wharton, Bernard Berenson and heaven knows who else on the international scene. Rudyard Kipling and Henry Adams ... I'd forgotten those two. But I fancy they were earlier.'

No answer.

Dorothy stirred the fire and fell to wondering if one day *The Times* would publish an obituary of the authoress of *The Golden Gong* and the series of related novels that would follow it. Her imagination toyed with various headings for the notice, settling finally on 'DOROTHY HENDERSON, Literary Novelist of Wide Appeal'.

'I'd love to win the GEMA,' she confessed. 'It's *the* prize, so far as I'm concerned.'

Ida lowered her book. The head oscillation began again, the face remaining frozen.

'The GEMA has never been won by a first novel,' she informed the woman who had supplied that piece of information.

'I know. But it could happen, Ida.'

'*Reste à savwahr.* When George Eliot endowed the prize, she said nothing that precludes a first novel from winning. Yours could be that first novel,' Ida allowed, not without a certain grace. She returned to the printed word, adding: 'I haven't read *The Golden Gong*, so I can't offer an opinion. All I can say is that it will have to be exceptional even to be nominated.'

'We'd spend the prize money on a tour of America. How does that appeal to you? I'd love to explore New England, where so many creative people came from, and New Orleans, and especially the Hollywood studios, where the great movies of the 1930s and '40s were made. Those films told stories that had a beginning, a middle and an end. They didn't rely for effect on gratuitous violence, raw sex, coarse language and a car chase. They revolved around strong plots and mature dialogue. And of course, the stars! – those magic people. No two were alike in voice, style or appearance, were they? What they had in common was individuality, good manners and sophistication, especially in regard to clothes.'

'I'd prefer to see Cynthia's summer residence in the South of France,' Ida said. 'America is too full of foreigners for my liking. There's no such thing as a real American.'

'I think, you know, that I'd be content with a review of *The Golden Gong* by A. J. C. Villiers. If ever the GEMA came my way, I'd like it to symbolise a body of work instead of one first-rate novel. But I'm fooling myself ... I'll be happy if *The Golden Gong* gets decent notices and has a moderate success.'

'A. J. C. Villiers reviews only one book a week,' Ida stated, this time parroting Mark Nolan, who claimed friendship with Arthur Villiers when in truth he'd never met him. 'As Literary Editor, Mr Villiers has first choice of everything publishers send in for review.'

Dorothy looked up at the clock.

'Rabbit is not to use the car ever again,' she announced. 'This is him now. I shall confiscate his keys and in future he can go to Arrowcross, when I choose to let him, on the train and pay his fare out of his allowance.'

Ida closed her book, removed her 'spectaculars', as Robin called them, and looked at Dorothy.

'What are you going to do to him?' she asked, warily.

'Wait and see,' Dorothy answered, on her way to the door.

* * *

Ida heard her say 'Get upstairs' through the closed door. When it opened again, Robin entered first with Dorothy hard on his heels. In the same moment, Ida's pose collapsed into unfettered laughter.

Robin was naked save for a short petticoat taken from among the surplus garments on Ida's bed. His face was powdered and daubed with streaks of lipstick. His wrists were tied behind his back.

'It's a spanking for my little man,' Dorothy stated. 'A command performance fit for a prince, if you see what I mean.'

Robin looked at Ida. She was pointing at him, her cheeks already wet with tears, her body already shaking.

Dorothy carried an upright chair to the centre of the room, sat down and guided her captive to her right side. She lifted the petticoat up to his waist, making Ida squeal like a schoolgirl and hide her eyes. When she peeped through her fingers, Dorothy was looking up at her husband and ordering him to bend over.

'Quickly! Get right across,' she snapped.

His eyes downcast, Robin let himself be helped forwards and downwards until his toes were touching the carpet at one side of the chair and his brow resting on it at the other.

'Don't dare try to escape. If you do, I'll send Ida to fetch the strap.'

But Ida was in no condition to fetch anything. She had checked her mirth long enough to stabilise herself and dab her eyes, but now she was off again, leaning backwards so that her feet left the floor, and pointing with renewed glee at Robin as he began jerking and squirming in response to the smacking. But with Dorothy's left arm round his waist, he was as much a prisoner as a man on the rack.

'Stop, stop, stop!' he cried, kicking his legs. 'Please, Dilly!'

But his wife, grinding her teeth, only slapped harder.

Suddenly she stopped. Robin went on jerking. Frowning, Dorothy tilted his body away from her abdomen. Then, at sight of the mess on her skirt, she sprang to her feet, tipping him onto the carpet.

'You filthy beast!' she hissed.

Ida rose, her laughter gone, as Dorothy set about him.

'Stop that! That's sadism!' she shouted.

But Dorothy was in a frenzy. With locked jaws and staring eyes, she stood over her twisting victim and kicked and kicked and kicked until Ida seized her from behind and dragged her off him.

'You crazy fool! D'you want to kill him?' she demanded.

She sank to her knees at Robin's side and untied his wrists, while Dorothy glared down at him in anger and disgust.

105

'Get up, Bobs. I'll help you,' Ida said.

Robin nodded. His eyes were closed, his freed hands pressed to his stomach.

'Bitch!' said Ida, as they turned their backs on Dorothy. 'Candy's right. You should have been a guard at Belsen.'

She had looped Robin's left arm round her shoulders and her right round his waist, and now she was walking him carefully out of the room and up the stairs, ignoring the ringing telephone.

Once in his bedroom, Ida removed the petticoat and steadied him while he got into his pyjamas. Her nursing experience, brief and inglorious though it had been, assisted her when it came to putting him to bed. She was cleaning his face when Dorothy appeared in the doorway.

'Max is dead,' she announced, coldly. 'That was Norah Blanchard. I'll have to attend the funeral on your behalf.'

Robin, on his back, was looking at the ceiling.

'Poor Panie Bracie!' he said, almost inaudibly. 'He was as lively as a flea this afternoon.'

'He collapsed on the terrace. A heart attack. He was dead before he hit the ground.'

'He wasn't good to me, but he wasn't bad either,' Robin sighed, his head lolling on the pillow. 'I'm sorry I can't be there to pay my respects. Hilary will miss him most. She was very fond of the Man of Wrath.'

'You're to say you were beaten up in the street. D'you understand?' Dorothy snapped at him. 'That's what I told Norah Blanchard. You were posting my letters this evening outside The Tracing Board when some drunks came out and demanded money. When you said you hadn't any, they knocked you down and started kicking you.'

Ida opened her lips to speak, but then checked herself.

'You can't describe your attackers,' Dorothy continued, 'which is why we haven't contacted the police. It was dark and they soon ran off. There were no witnesses.'

'She's got it all worked out,' Robin murmured, managing a smile and a blink at Ida Prince. 'But what do I say if I'm asked about the temperature on the Air Ministry roof?'

He winced as he eased his back off the mattress. He would be as stiff as a board next day.

'I'll sit with you tonight,' Ida told him, huskily, already enjoying the prospect of holding her patient's hand through the quiet hours. 'If you're running a temperature in the morning, I'll send for Doctor Arlen.'

Dorothy turned contemptuously on her heel and went up to the schoolroom, slamming the door.

The conspirators exchanged smiles.

'Are you going to spill the beans to Dotty?' Robin asked.

'You've already spilt your half. I just wish you could have seen her face when the truth dawned! I think the whole of her married life passed before her.'

They kissed.

'It took a long time, but I finally got you across her knee,' Ida murmured, with her lips brushing his. 'I'm only sorry it ended in a kicking.'

'She'd have given me that anyway. Breaking out of prison and taking a motor vehicle without the owner's consent would have been a marvellous excuse for knocking me about. But she'd have waited till you were out of the house.'

'You were very brave. I love and respect you for what you did.'

'What about the rest of the beans? It'll mean the end for you.'

'I'll tell her just before she leaves for the funeral.'

* * *

Norah came to the kitchen door as Dorothy's taxi turned round in the cobbled yard to begin its return journey to Wall Town Station. She looked as cross as she had sounded when talking to Dorothy over the telephone.

'If you want anything, you'll have to forage for yourself,' she said, waving aside Dorothy's greeting. 'I sent Mrs Trapnell home at twelve and I'm going upstairs to rest till the cars come.'

Dorothy wasn't hungry. With a cup of tea at her side and the *Wall Town News* open in her lap, she passed a cheerless hour in the drawing room. A hot spell, as brief as it had been unexpected, had ended abruptly, leaving it chilly enough to make her wish she had brought a coat to wear over the invariable black suit and white blouse. All she could do was keep her gloves on as well as the new black hat with the short veil that she found rather becoming. Nobody came or went in the yard or the house, where the only sound was the leisurely and relaxing tick-tock of the longcase clock in the hall.

Eventually, the hearse arrived, with one mourners' car in rear. As Dorothy rose, Norah came downstairs with the promptitude of a boarder rallying to the dinner gong, making obvious the fact that she had been waiting and watching in her bedroom.

The driver shut them in.

'Where is Hilary?' Dorothy asked.

'At the farrier's,' Norah snapped.

'Is no one else coming?'

'The Nolans are in Venice. Everyone else is dead.'

The five minute journey was accomplished in silence, each woman feigning preoccupation with the cottages and farms beyond her window.

'I don't like the look of those black clouds over there,' Dorothy confessed, anxiously, as they prepared to alight.

Norah disregarded the comment. She stepped forward to kiss Flora Tenbury, who, widowed herself now, was waiting in the porch. She and Dorothy took no notice of one another.

The organ droned in the little Norman church, with its tolling bell and oaken pews. Arran and Blanch Clark, who gratefully made room for her, were the only mourners Dorothy recognised. There were several London faces, some local hewers of wood and drawers of water in navy blue serge and check shirts, and a scattering of camphorated dowagers and brittle retired officers, their watery eyes straying ever and again to the flower-decked coffin in the aisle. In this same church, Arran had given Dorothy away to an immensely proud Robin; but the minister who had united them had long since departed for the country beyond the hill. The present incumbent knew nothing of the breath-catching sight of Dorothy Hatfield entering in purest white and had met the deceased but once. He wisely confined himself to a textbook eulogy of 'our lost brother, Walter Maxwell Blanchard', before moving to a reading from Ecclesiastes, which ended with: 'Then shall the dust return to the earth as it was and the spirit shall return unto God who gave it'.

The first dabs of rain spattered the coffin as it began its descent into the grave that already contained the mortal remains of Max's first wife. Presently came a flash of lightning and a low growl of thunder. By the time Dorothy resumed her seat in the black Humber Pullman, having said goodbye to the admiring Clarks and turned her back on Norah, the rain had become steady.

'There's someone still to come,' she told the driver, as he began to close the door.

'Mrs Blanchard told me to say she'll follow later in Lady Tenbury's car, madam,' he answered.

Once in the yard, Dorothy ran across the cobbles as quickly as four-inch heels would permit, unaware that she was being watched. But the kitchen door was locked. She beat on it with her small fists while the slanting rain whipped the backs of her legs. No one came. Panicking, she ran with bowed head and contorted face to the front door. Locked. Moving to the terrace, she rattled the French windows, but they didn't yield.

The mourners' car had turned and gone and there was no sign of any other vehicle on the drive or in the yard. Saturated now and with water running into her eyes and mouth, she dashed across to the stable block, entering by the open double doors and wishing she'd had the presence of mind to ask the driver to take her to Wall Town.

Hilary's school horses had been and gone, leaving all save four of the high-sided stalls empty. A sky-splitting crack of thunder chased Dorothy into the nearest of them, where she stood ankle deep in straw, shivering with cold and terror, unable to take her eyes off the curtain of water clattering down from an overflowing gutter above the doors.

The air was pungent with the smell of ammonia. The sounds from the occupied stalls were the soft sounds of horses snatching hay from nets, horses munching, horses making small movements on straw or peat bedding. Then, as thunder ripped through the clouds again, and the downpour suddenly hissed and drummed with yet greater intensity, Dorothy became aware of approaching footsteps.

Horror seized her. The steps were measured, unhurried, flat-heeled.

'Who is it?' she cried.

She shrank back like a threatened cat as the footfalls came nearer. In a moment, someone would appear round the partition.

'Who is it?' she sobbed.

No answer.

She screamed, her trembling hands pressed to her cheeks, her back to the brick wall.

It was Hilary.

'Oh, thank God it's only you!' Dorothy gasped, overwhelmed with relief. 'Why didn't you say?'

Hilary stood watching her, motionless and inscrutable in scuffed jackboots, stretch breeches that needed washing, a well-used hacking jacket and a maroon shirt open at the neck.

'The Tracing Board has been closed for more than a month,' she said, in a level voice. 'The pillarbox has been moved. It's now outside Ellery Mansions, where Maud Barclay lives.'

Dorothy's lips opened.

'Robin didn't know. He can't have done. Otherwise he wouldn't have gone there,' she babbled.

Hilary came into the stall. There was a cutting whip in her hand. She spoke quietly.

'It was you who knocked him about. You've been beating my father for years, haven't you? You didn't think anyone knew, except yourself and your trapped victim, who stuck it for my sake and because he's too fine a man ever to hit a woman. I didn't suspect anything myself until a few weeks ago, when I noticed cane marks on him when he was undressing with his door partly open. Afterwards, I recalled the bruises I'd seen from time to time and the limp that he had trouble explaining away. It's your business to concoct stories, but the one about The Tracing Board suffers from poor research.'

Hilary advanced, tapping the straight, flexible whip on the palm of her left hand.

'Hilary! Hilary! Hilary, listen to me! Your father *wanted* me to beat and humiliate him. You're too young to understand, dear. I couldn't believe it myself until Ida drove me to Waterloo Station this morning. Hilary, listen! Ida was Stella –'

Shrieking, Dorothy doubled up and turned away, shielding her head with her arms as the thrashing began. Calmly and systematically, evincing neither pity nor pleasure, the girl whipped her stepmother's shoulders, buttocks, thighs and calves; and she went on whipping, unmoved by her victim's howls, until the Land Rover was heard lumbering into the yard.

Dorothy was on her knees now, hugging Hilary's thighs and sobbing on the edge of complete breakdown. Her nylons were out at the knees and laddered throughout their length. Her skirt and jacket, blacker than their normal black from the soaking they had received, were covered with bits of straw.

'Some louts were waiting for you when you got back from the church,' Hilary said, expressionlessly. 'They demanded to be let into the house. When you said you hadn't a key, they made a mess of you before driving off in a car. You staggered over here, looking as you do now, and I found you lying dazed in the bedding. Stick to that and I'll do the same – unless you prefer to tell the truth. Camilla will drive you to the station. As you are.'

CHAPTER TEN

Dorothy stayed overnight at the Station Hotel in Wall Town, where she was just in time to buy nylons and an umbrella before the shops closed. The little black hat was ruined. She dined in her room, borrowed the hotel iron to press her skirt and blouse, and had her shoes and jacket dried in the kitchen. Next morning, outwardly none the worse for her ordeal, she returned to Waterloo by train and from there by taxi to Willow Square.

Ida Prince and Robin greeted her with broad smiles on the topmost of the wide steps leading up to the front door. The warmth of their welcome contained a degree of nervous defiance, making them seem like guests who had moved the furniture round in their hostess's absence. Dorothy guessed that The Tramps had been in her house. They had not been at the funeral, although they were now resident at Bytheway House.

'Thanks for calling us from Wall Street last night,' Ida began, not noticing her slip of the tongue, 'but you should have let me come for you in the car. Shouldn't she, Bobs?'

'You know Dilpickle – a law unto herself. Like poor Jesus, she's the same yesterday, today and forever. You girls go and talk while I crack on with the lunch,' Robin said, wafting away into his kitchen. 'I'll ask about the funeral later.'

Bright dance music from the Grundig Bergamo filled the ground floor. Ida lowered the volume as she and Dorothy sat down in the drawing room. The atmosphere was so carefree that Dorothy felt herself a stranger in her own home. It was as if shuttered windows had been thrown open to admit fresh air, sunshine and the sounds of living. So disconcerting was this to Dorothy that she could control her agitation only by reminding herself that Ida and Robin would be gone next day.

'You look nice,' she told Ida, stiffly. 'I haven't seen those clothes before.'

'We went to Ketter's yesterday and spent a little of Robin's money. I made him buy a couple of decent suits after a heavy hint from Candy and Derek that casual clothes won't be welcome at Bytheway House,' Ida said.

She was her natural self again – the Ida whom Robin had known as Stella, the Ida with whom Dorothy had fallen in love. All evidence of copycat artificiality had vanished, along with the crust of grease paint and the bottle-bottoms reading glasses. Her short red hair and lovely emerald eyes were now complemented by a green accordion pleated skirt, a yellow-and-brown candy stripe blouse, whisky-coloured tights and brown suede court shoes. She led the conversation in her slow, sore-throat voice, as careless now of accent and diction as she was dismissive of French and Cynthia Justin Bourn. It would be a long time before she could bring herself to admit that she had been making a fool of herself, and longer still before she finally parted with her uniform.

'I was going to sling it on the charity heap, but Bobs asked me to keep it for special occasions,' she confessed, smiling as she tilted her head back slightly. 'If you understand what I mean.'

Dorothy looked away, her features tightened by the acid resentment of a woman long deceived. Years before, she had adopted her uniform in the belief that its severity would make her unattractive to her husband. On the drive to Waterloo, she had learned from Ida that it had achieved precisely the opposite effect.

'Men who came to me in Scrub Hill – "clients", as Billy Prince made me call them – had preferences as to how I dressed, same as they had certain routines they wanted me to follow,' Ida explained, capable at this remove of appreciating the amusing side of it. 'Robin always wanted me in black and white, with high heels. I was his wicked governess. What's the matter?'

Dorothy was crying.

'I can't get over it,' she gasped. 'You were nothing more than a prostitute.'

'Hey! Hang on! Don't you call me a tom.'

'Well, what else were you? If entertaining men while your husband sits in the kitchen isn't prostitution, what is it?'

Ida was on her feet.

'Are you suggesting I had intercourse with them?' she demanded.

'Keep your voice down, please.'

'Are you? Answer me!'

'Well, yes. How can I think otherwise? Men don't pay women just to cane them and treat them like naughty boys.'

'Don't they? Don't they? That's all you know. When were you last in Soho?'

'I've no idea.'

'Right! Well, you're coming with me this afternoon and I'm going to show you the postcard adverts in shop windows. "Miss Birch Gives Lessons in Advanced English". "Attractive Schoolmistress Takes Difficult Pupils". It's known as Discipline, or CP, which is short for corporal punishment. But it isn't prostitution.'

'I'm not convinced.'

Ida opened her mouth to speak, as Robin's blond head came round the door.

'Lunchies,' he announced, perkily.

'Not yet, Robin. We're talking,' Ida responded, brusquely. 'Leave us, please.'

She turned swiftly to Dorothy, who was getting up and dabbing her eyes with an embroidered handkerchief.

'Listen! We're not leaving this room, Dilly, until you say you believe me. I may not go to church, but I'm still a Catholic and I swear before Almighty God and the Hail Mary that I've never in my life let any man touch me except Billy Prince. Now d'you believe me?'

Dorothy nodded.

'Say it. Say you do,' Ida insisted.

'I believe you, Ida.'

'If I'd been on the game, Dilly, I'd never have told you what I've told you so far. I didn't *have* to tell you I was Stella. If you must know, I was getting back at you for the way you treated

114

Robin. I wanted you to know that he'd been laughing behind your back for years. But if I'd thought for one moment you'd take me for a tom, I'd never have said nothing and I'm sorry now I did.'

'I'm hungry. Let's have lunch, Ida.'

Egg soup was followed by baked gammon with apricot stuffing, spinach and buttered potatoes, with college pudding as dessert. With the main course, Robin served an inexpensive claret.

'For you, Dilly?' he ventured.

To his surprise, she nodded.

'We'll make a boozer of her yet, won't we, Ida?' he suggested, with a smile and a blink. 'Funny, isn't it, that you and Dilly very nearly came face to face on the night of the road accident? I've often thought about it. Could you have fixed us up with an abortionist?'

Dorothy glared at him.

'Shut up!' Ida shouted. 'That subject is closed and don't ever mention it again. D'you understand? Are you all right, Dilly?'

'Just a little unsteady, that's all,' Dorothy answered.

She talked about the torrential rain that had followed Max's burial, of how she had got drenched just running from the car into Nellie's kitchen. Neither she nor Hilary Blanchard ever said a word about the whipping. To explain her bruises and the flattened hat, Dorothy pretended that she had stumbled in the cobbles and fallen headlong.

'I'll go up to bed in a minute,' she added, quietly. 'I feel worn out all of a sudden.'

'Let me put a coal fire in your room,' Ida said. 'You like a coal fire. After dark, you can watch the flames make patterns on the ceiling.'

Dorothy nodded her thanks.

'Will you live at Bytheway House?' she asked, indifferently.

'We've got a choice – live with Candy and Derek or live with Norah and Hilary,' Robin replied. 'I think we'll settle for Arrowcross, but Auntie makes the decisions.'

'Working as well as living with the Comforts may not be a good thing. Besides, Norah seems to want us, and Hilary and me are like sisters,' Ida said.

'Hilary and I,' Dorothy corrected, mechanically. 'I see the motel block is going ahead. It was in the *Wall Town News*.'

'It's with the hotel in mind that we've decided to form a partnership, instead of being the Comforts' employees. The four of us are going to see a solicitor in Wall Town next week,' Ida explained.

'Candy and Derek came here to lunch yesterday,' Robin said, as though nothing in the world could have been more ordinary. 'They were in town for a meeting with Reklaw's free trade people.'

'We've now got financial help from the brewery to build the motel block on condition we stock their beers, wines and spirits,' said Ida. 'The four of us went over everything after luncheon and it's all coming together very nicely.'

'I've seen it developing, of course,' Dorothy said, without malice or bitterness. 'It doesn't take Philip Marlowe to detect where you both sat when I was out of the house. There wasn't room for a matchbox between the pair of you on the sofa facing the television screen. As for your meetings with The Tramps, I don't know much about motorcars, but I do know which of the dials counts the mileage and I know how much further Broseley is from The Orchid Room.'

Her listeners, avoiding her eyes, shifted about uncomfortably. Ida was scratching her knee, Robin his face.

Dorothy asked him if he wanted a divorce.

'It would be neater,' he agreed.

'I want us to be always friends, Dilly,' Ida said, huskily. She placed one of her big hands on Dorothy's, but Dorothy drew hers from beneath it. 'If you won't come to see us, can we come to see you?'

'I'm moving to Paris as soon as *The Golden Gong* is in print. I don't know whereabouts yet.'

Ida rose.

'I'll go and put that fire in your room,' she said, conclusively.

'You sound very confident of publication, old girl,' Robin commented, smiling at his wife. 'More wine?'

Dorothy shook her head.

'I'm forty,' she stated. 'If I haven't come of age now as a novelist, I never shall. I've put every ounce of experience and creativity I can muster into *The Golden Gong*. If it's rejected,

Robin, I don't know what I shall do; because I can't do better.'

'It won't be rejected, Dillyflower.'

'No. I don't think it will.'

*   *   *

Robin and Ida delayed their departure, postponing the solicitor's appointment until Dorothy was able to get up and see to herself again. In the interval, they bought a smart red Riley Kestrel. Having no use for the Consul 375, which she had intended giving them, Dorothy asked Mark Nolan if he would accept it as a gift. He had done so much for her, from guiding the development of Mary Orchard to regularly checking her royalty account at Marjorie d'Or. As it happened, his wife was learning to drive, so the Consul was a timely and welcome present. Robin, when told, wondered what sort of a driver Sarah would make, with her white poodle, blue rinse, and narrowed eyes fluttering behind spectacles in fancy frames. He doubted if she would ever get out of second gear.

Norah had wired Mark in Venice to tell of Max's death and Mark had had a lengthy telephone talk with her on returning to Norris Green. The dissolution of the *ménage à trois* hadn't come as a complete surprise, since he had detected friction building between Ida and Dorothy for some time, but he was too sophisticated to broach the subject at Willow Square.

Dorothy made no direct reference to it either. The outward signs included the silence that was everywhere and the military neatness of the schoolroom. Ida's typewriter was covered and there were no papers on Dorothy's spotless pink blotter. Gently, because she still looked pale and depleted, Mark asked if she had finished the rewrite of *Connie's First Term*.

She brought coffee and biscuits from the kitchenette and they settled themselves within range of the gas fire.

'You're going to be angry with me, Mark. We've had quite an upheaval, beginning with Max and ending with my bout of influenza or whatever it was. It felt so much like the Black Death that I expected to hear a voice in the square bidding us bring out our dead. But I promise, promise, promise that I'll have it for you at the end of the month.'

117

'That's time enough, Dilly. Don't worry about it.'

'What about the manuscript from the policeman, Mark? Any good? I rather liked it myself.'

'No good for Marjorie d'Or, so I've left it with van Doren. I'm sure he'll take it.'

'Another addition to your Family of Writers. And the novel by the Liverpool lass? Did you find time to read it between visits to Florian's and Harry's Bar?'

Mark's grin began as a sneer.

'Ivy Robinson! Lissern! You wrote it yourself, you scally-wag,' he thundered, joyfully. 'It's got Dorothy Blanchard stamped all over it.'

'I thought if I passed it off as the work of a stranger, you'd be more impartial.'

'Mary Orchard has never been sent a novel like *The Golden Gong* in her life.'

'Are you saying it's good?'

'Too good for Mark Moron. I'm used to skimming through manuscripts to see if they'll sell, not to wondering if they'll be nominated for the GEMA or reviewed by Arthur Villiers. I'm no more qualified to judge adult fiction than Eddie Lombard. What I've done is leave your novel with Duncan Macalister at Sandrew Morath, and what you must do is ring his secretary for an appointment.'

'Oh, Mark! Mark, you're lovely! You'll still be my agent, Mark, won't you? I don't want to deal direct with Mr Macalister or anyone else.'

'We'll talk about that when the time comes, Dilly. Mean-while, don't call a press conference at the Dorchester on the strength of an interview with the one-armed bandit. He may buy your book and he may not.'

Dorothy sat forward eagerly.

'Give me your honest opinion of *The Golden Gong*, Mark.'

'My honest opinion? OK. It's beautifully written. You have a gift for *le mot juste* that Raymond Chandler would have en-vied. Your characters spring to life – especially Hap Sanderlin, the old head of the clan – and they live on after we close the book. But I don't think it'll be a blockbuster.'

'Mark dear, I don't want it to be. I don't want to see posers ostentatiously reading it on Underground trains. What you've just said has delighted me. I want *The Golden Gong* to be cherished by people who love books. I want to see it make friends slowly and steadily until, twenty years from now, it joins five succeeding novels to form my Collected Edition.'

Cynthia Justin Bourn had called her collected Lampeter novels the Dartmoor Edition, whilst Henry James's American publisher had reissued the best of James's writings as the New York Edition. Dorothy Henderson's six novels, Dorothy Blanchard decided, would form the Cluny Edition, since Cluny was the place in France near which she intended to settle. She saw them bound in quarter leather, with navy blue boards, gold blocking and pale blue marbled end papers.

'Hey there! You with the stars in your eyes,' Mark exclaimed, smiling as he passed his hand in front of Dorothy's face. 'I'm afraid I've got to bring you back to earth with a bump, my lady, by reminding you that you promised me a new Mary Orchard for Eddie's spring list. We must have at least three chapters and a synopsis before Christmas.'

Dorothy drew a long breath and slowly exhaled. She had completely forgotten her commitment.

'Can't I have a leg amputated instead?'

'Oh, come off it! What's happened to my Dorothy? Mary Orchard can knock off a forty thousand word Walker's Croft in six weeks. I'm giving you as many months. Well, almost.'

'Mark, I'll need someone who can type and take dictation. A temp. I'm sure you know someone.'

'I have my contacts. She calls herself Gee, because she doesn't like being called Gladys. I'll get her to give you a ring.'

Dorothy was sharing the last of the coffee between the two cups.

'How's Lucy these days?' she asked. 'I rather like her name, you know – it's so feminine. I was nearly called Lucy myself.'

'She's doing fine. At the moment, van Doren is trying to woo her away from Eddie. You all have your hour at the feast, Dilly, from Angela Brazil to Felicity Hatna.'

'And from Mary Orchard to Lucy Reynolds.'

'You've only yourself to blame. You've ignored Eddie's pleas for a return to swift movement and Ruth Berrido's advice to come up to date. Let your last book be a valediction we can all be proud of – you, me and Eddie. Let me have material without a pillow fight in it. Bring in Elvis and The Beatles, no matter how much they may offend you. Change Mabel and Millicent to Sandra and Debbie. Show us all that Mary Orchard can still top the bill if she wants to.'

'All right. You've thrown down the gauntlet.'

'I know what you want, Dilly, and I hope with all my heart that you get it. But don't blow your brains out if you don't, because I can use them elsewhere. I'm diversifying. That's the buzz word, my daughters tell me. I'm adding radio and television to my literary agenting, so I'll be on the look-out for original scripts, dialogue writers and people who can make sensitive adaptations of the classics. So don't throw my card away.'

'I'll never do that, Mark. And shall I tell you something? I still have the original card – the one Robin brought to me in my writing room when you first came to Great Homer Street.'

* * *

Despite her longevity as an established writer, Dorothy had never seen the inside of a book publisher's premises. Her imagination told her that the Hammersmith offices of Marjorie d'Or were a warren of threadbare rooms, whilst those of Sandrew Morath in College Square, Bloomsbury, betokened solid achievement and membership of White's. She was more or less accurate on both counts.

'It's all about to change, Mrs Blanchard,' Duncan Macalister explained, once he had seated and settled her. 'Next time we see each other, we'll be clattering about on several acres of thermoplastic tiles in a new block in Hoseside which we'll share with a subsidiary of ours called Marjorie d'Or Adventure Library. You probably haven't heard of them. They publish juvenile fiction.'

'Mary Orchard and Lucy Reynolds.'

'That sort of thing. Anyhow, I've decided to retire, Mrs Blanchard. I'm a little too old for blue jeans and a leather jacket.'

An international corporation, newly arrived in the book trade, had recently bought Sandrew Morath Holdings and had already made clear its impatience with coal fires and Heal's furniture, likewise with the avuncular editors who

cherished them. Bordered Wilton carpets with brown linoleum surrounds and handsome bindings behind leaded glass
would soon be abandoned in favour of open plan accommodation where the high and the humble would work within
earshot of one another's Christian names. The highest and
least humble would be out of reach of authors and employees
alike in the carpeted hush of the penthouse executive suite,
complete with directors' dining room and relaxing roof garden.

'I'm sure you're glad to be going,' Dorothy said, smiling.
'Retirement can be so rewarding, provided we plan for it.'

'Oh, I agree. If it amounts to no more than watching
television and taking the dog to the corner, it must be hell on
earth for a sensitive soul.'

Macalister's had been among the London faces at Max's
funeral. He was tall and spare, with healthy skin, and
blue eyes that brightened with his frequent and disarming
smile. Dorothy liked his voice, which contained a caressing
quality when he was talking to women. One empty sleeve of his
grey flannel suit was tucked into a side pocket. He wore a
flower in his lapel, as Max had always done when formally
dressed.

Dorothy asked if he had spent his life in publishing.

He had.

'When I came down from Merton in 1928, I went to Werner
Laurie for a few months, then came here. It was like coming
home. The first thing that impressed me was the fact that the
partners shook hands every morning. They read every letter
that came in and signed every letter that went out. They were
in daily contact with every employee, from the commis-
sionaire to the warehouseman, and they met every author
whose work they published. This room was Harry Morath's.'

The leather-topped desk had a raised centre portion, the
hinged lid of which sloped towards the occupant. A manuscript lay on the lid.

'Martin Sandrew's office was through the door behind me.
Those rooms we passed walking along the corridor were
occupied by readers, editors and secretaries. Some have survived and are now at Hoseside, but they may not like tele-
phones ringing all around them and a tea trolley rattling
through twice a day. They won't have a steward to make up

the fires, polish the brasses and serve coffee at eleven and tea at four, as they had here.'

'You make it sound like paradise lost, Mr Macalister.'

'Well, I liked it, Mrs Blanchard, but I'm an old fogy and old fogies reminisce. You want to talk about your delightful novel and so do I. I understand you'd like Mr Nolan to represent you?'

Dorothy smiled and nodded – too overjoyed to assemble a reply before Macalister continued speaking.

'A contract will be ready in a day or two, and Mr Nolan will go through it with you. Then we must move quickly into jacket design, type face, dedicatee and what not, because I want your book in our Christmas list. Among the good things to arise from the take-over are faster processing and much more positive and imaginative advertising. Martin, and more so Harry, considered publicity a touch vulgar. Good notices in the *Observer* and the *TLS* were all that mattered; but my new masters, Mrs Blanchard, will want to make a celebrity of you.'

Duncan paused, responding with a calming smile to Dorothy's visible alarm.

'I'm speaking of radio and television interviews, book signings and that sort of thing. Don't let it bother you. Let's get that contract signed before you kick against anything. One thing they've tripped over, and I must agree with them – your title. *The Passive Voice*. We feel it's a little too passive, if you'll forgive the pun, and we suggest changing it to *Mitten's Luck*.'

'*The Passive Voice* is not the title of my novel. The title of my novel is *The Golden Gong*.'

Frowning, and darting a flustered glance at a second manuscript on his desk, Macalister leaned forward and put on his spectacles to look again at the title page of the manuscript in front of him.

'You're Hilary Blanchard?' he ventured, cautiously.

'No. I'm Dorothy Blanchard.'

Macalister's hand went slowly to his face. He placed the thumb against his temple and the fingers against his brow, where they hid his eyes. A deep blush rose from the white collar of his pink shirt and climbed to the roots of his hair.

'Mrs Blanchard,' he began, 'I've made a dreadful mistake. A week or so before he died, Max Blanchard handed me the manuscript of *The Passive Voice* and asked if I'd read it with a view to making an offer. Some time later, Mr Nolan, whom I've never met, left the manuscript of *The Golden Gong* with our receptionist, marked for my attention. I was too busy to meet him, what with the impending move to Hoseside. I'm very much afraid, Mrs Blanchard, that I've mixed up your novel with Hilary's. Are you related?'

Suddenly more dead than alive, Dorothy could only stare at and through Macalister in searing hatred. To cover his embarrassment, he picked up the telephone to ask for tea to be sent up, then quietly resumed his apologies and commiserations, explaining that his secretary must have mistaken Dorothy's telephone call for Hilary's response to his letter inviting her to make an appointment. Facing the black-clad woman, still jaded from her illness, he felt he was consoling a mother who had lost her only child.

Dorothy asked tonelessly if he had read *The Golden Gong*.

He had. And it was splendid. Truly splendid.

'You tell a story that is organic, not contrived, and your writing is among the most vivid and sensitive I've met in my life.'

'But you're not going to publish it.'

Macalister hesitated, at war with himself.

'I do wish I could make you an offer, Mrs Blanchard, and even up to a couple of years ago I probably could. Yours is a quality novel – what we call a literary novel – and as such would have a modest but steady sale over a period of years. Fine! But my new masters are looking for fiction that will have a brief but spectacular career, not only in print, but on television too.'

'I shall try other publishers,' Dorothy said, coldly.

'Please do, Mrs Blanchard, and let me recommend three or four while you drink your tea. We are not all of us in the grip of the supermarket mentality, but I fancy we soon shall be.'

Macalister placed a compliments slip, printed side down, on Dorothy's manuscript, weighted it at one corner and began writing intermittently with an Eversharp propelling pencil.

123

While he pondered and wrote, Dorothy, aware now that her hatred of him was fruitless and unreasonable, asked if there were any criticisms he would like to make of *The Golden Gong*.

'The subject matter is the problem,' he replied, as if dictating to a secretary. 'I don't know if you've ever heard of a novelist by the name of Cynthia Justin Bourn? It has been said of Henry James that he's the world's most celebrated unread author, and really the same could be said of Miss Bourn. With *The Golden Gong*, you seem to be setting off on a pilgrimage through the enclosed world of social distinctions that these two novelists delineated in loving detail. But do readers want to go with you?'

Dorothy, watching him steadily, said nothing.

'As a publisher, I have to make a commercial decision,' he went on. 'The days are gone when London publishing was a gentlemen's club in which only cads admitted to making money. A novel that sold two thousand copies in hardback and a further three thousand in soft was perfectly acceptable. Miss Bourn made very little money for Sandrew Morath, but the partners were proud of their association with a novelist whose books were said to be in every country house in England. All that belongs to the past, Mrs Blanchard. Today at Sandrew Morath, it's money first, money second and money third. Our new chairman has described prestige as a riderless horse.'

'I don't think we're talking about anything so petty and ignoble as prestige,' Dorothy retorted, testily, her hatred returning. 'I think we're talking about publishers who put quality before quantity and considered it part of their duty to promote literacy and good taste.'

'Well, perhaps you're right, Mrs Blanchard. Here are the names of other publishers, but there's no need to mention me or Sandrew Morath.'

They stood up and shook hands and Macalister continued to hold Dorothy's for a few moments before releasing it.

'You have considerable talent, Mrs Blanchard, but you're wasting it on material that has less appeal today than ever it had. It's as though Michelangelo were painting the ceiling of Ketter's instead of the Sistine Chapel. Unfortunately, I don't think you're the sort of person who will take advice.'

'I can't write to order, if that's what you mean. I can't go against my instincts.'

'Good luck with those names I've given you, and do remember that publishers make mistakes, myself included.'

'You seem extremely confident of the success of my step-daughter's novel. I can only conclude, from what you've told me of your new masters' requirements, that it'll be the sort of bestselling slab that one leaves in the train at King's Cross. What sort of sales are you expecting for this first attempt by an inexperienced girl?'

'You're immersed in the past, Mrs Blanchard, so I'll take a pointer from the past. If the great circulating libraries, such as Boots or Smiths' were still with us today, they would take six copies of *Mitten's Luck* for each of their branches. I repeat, each of their branches.'

'How many would they take of *The Golden Gong*?'

'One. I'm hurting you, Mrs Blanchard, but I'm hurting you in order to help you. Don't go without your manuscript.'

CHAPTER ELEVEN

It was as if her vitality had drained away, leaving only a vile and corrosive residue. Restless and fretful, seeking to blunt her awareness with repetitive housework, she could think of nothing save her lost child, her aborted career as Dorothy Henderson, and the emergence of Hilary Blanchard.

'The little slyboots!' she hissed, with flared nostrils. 'She kept her face shut about *Mitten's Luck* all right. Tight shut.'

'As you did about *The Golden Gong*, Dilly,' Mark countered, gently. 'The Blanchard women are noted for their secrecy. Not even Norah knew about *Mitten's Luck* till last weekend. Max was first into the secret. Hilary told him only a few days before he died, because she didn't know how to go about getting it published. I can imagine what happened next. Can't you hear Panie Bracie, after treating Duncan to lunch at The Rag, putting on his broadest Lancashire and saying, "'Ere! Publish this if you want to go on being a guest gun at Arrowcross"?'

Dorothy was not amused. She had been staring at nothing through the schoolroom window, tapping her pencil on her thumbnail, and now she turned and walked dejectedly to her desk and sat down. The manuscript of *The Golden Gong* lay on her blotter, where it had lain since her return from Sandrew Morath. Mark had crossed out the by-line Ivy Robinson and written Dorothy Blanchard beneath it. On his card, stapled to the title page, he had written 'Recommend purchase. Mrs Blanchard 'phoning for appt.'

'When did you know about this novel of Hilary's?' Dorothy asked, venomously.

'Not till Sunday night, when Sarah and I were getting into the car to come home. We'd said goodbye to Norah in the drawing room, because she felt a cold coming on and didn't want to come out into the night air. We were having a few last words with Hilary through the car window when she produced a letter from Macalister inviting her to London to discuss her novel. I said: "What novel?" She said: "Oh, I'll explain later, Uncle Mark. Will you come with me? I won't know what to say." I took the letter and rang Duncan next morning to say I'd be representing Miss Blanchard. He was out and his secretary had already moved to Hoseside, but the girl I spoke to said she'd see Mr Macalister got my message. Next thing Duncan called me up at home – deeply embarrassed, because by then you'd already been in to see him.'

'He thinks *Mitten's Luck* will be the greatest thing since powered flight. What do you think?'

'I haven't read it, Dilly.'

'Macalister didn't surely mention his gaff in Hilary's presence?'

'Not a word. Not a hint. Duncan's a great professional, Dorothy, which makes his blunder all the more pitiable. As he said to me after the interview, he's never known a coincidence like this in nearly fifty years in publishing. I doubt if anyone has.'

'I'll make some tea,' Dorothy muttered.

'Who d'you think is slipping into his chair as Editorial Director?' Mark called out, while Dorothy was clattering about in the kitchenette.

'Eddie Lombard?'

'Right. I lunched with him yesterday. He took me to Olivelli's. Mantovani was at the next table. It's the end of a long association for Eddie and me, but of course we'll keep in touch. His successor at Marjorie d'Or will be his understudy, Muriel Lint.'

'I think we once talked to each other over the 'phone. It may have been about illustrations. *Connie's First Term* is ready, by the way. It's on the hall table.'

'Bless you. How did you get on with Gee? Gee Whiz.'

'I'm sorry, Mark, I couldn't stand her. She sat there gaping and grinning at me. I paid her for a full week, but got rid of her after three days. I did the *Connie* rewrite at night, working in the drawing room with pencil and rubber, then sleeping till lunch time, like Proust. For some reason, Mark, I can't work up here any more. The words just won't come.'

'Will you need a replacement for Gee Whiz?'

Dorothy sank down, sighing, onto the sofa, and shook her head in despair.

'I'm afraid so, Mark. I'm also afraid I'll have to go on being Mary Orchard for the rest of my life. My God! At the mere thought of it, I feel buried alive.'

'I've already got just the right lady lined up for you – Olivia Kingsley-Beaumont. She and Oswald, her husband, have joined our circle of friends since I started my move into broadcasting. Oswald is a television producer and Olivia is a publishers' maid-of-all-work. She's been editing, ghosting, indexing and cleaning up manuscripts for years. At the moment, she's completing a research assignment at Frederick Muller.'

'Why should a woman of her standing want to come here?'

'Olivia likes variety and she likes helping people. She'll be encouraging without being in any way intrusive. She's spent her life among creative people and she understands their problems.'

'What have you told her about me?' Dorothy asked, warily.

'Only that Mary Orchard needs patient and sympathetic support. No gawping. No grinning. She knows nothing about Dorothy Blanchard and *The Golden Gong*, if that's what you're thinking.'

Mark suspected that Dorothy was on the edge of a nervous breakdown. He believed that the company of an educated and articulate woman, albeit for only a few hours a day, could save her from it. He had taken Olivia into his confidence regarding the future of Mary Orchard, emphasising that Dorothy would have to be nudged into heeding the advice that he and Ruth Berrido had given her.

He was mindful too of the threat posed by Eddie's successor at Marjorie d'Or. Muriel Lint, already installed in the Hoseside fastness, had quickly emerged from Eddie's shadow as a hostile and calculating young woman, permanently trousered and with a penchant for four-letter words. In the course of a brief interview, in which it became clear that they didn't like one another, she had told Mark to find new talent, dismissing

Mary Orchard as "an individual high on my hit list". He had returned to his car irritated by her manner, especially her habit of saying "Momma knows best" and following the assumption with an unpleasant little grunt. Muriel had made him glad he was diversifying and even hopeful that Lucy Reynolds would succumb to van Doren's blandishments. Van Doren had hinted to Mark that he might try to poach Mary Orchard as well, but was van Doren aware of her declining popularity?

'Look to your past for quality and to the present for material, Dorothy,' Mark urged, quietly.

It upset him to see her so distressed by the rejection of *The Golden Gong* and the necessity of persisting as Mary Orchard.

'I've always liked you, Dilly, always respected you,' he went on. 'I love your honesty and loyalty and I want to go on helping you. These publishers Duncan has suggested – my advice is to forget them for the time being. Each of them will keep *The Golden Gong* for six or more weeks while they make a decision. Try agents instead. I don't mean the beads-and-tweeds variety, with a stone house in the Cotswolds and the kids away at school: those women are only playing at it. Established London agents are what you need. They know where to place a writer's work and you'll get a decision and possibly helpful advice as well within a fortnight. Above all, Dilly, don't despair. The world hasn't come to an end just because one man with one arm has declined to publish your novel.'

Dorothy nodded, aware that she must soon gather herself together if she were to retain the will to carry on.

'I'll do as you say, Mark,' she stated. 'I shall start bombarding agents this very afternoon.'

'Only one at a time, remember! Have you a spare copy of *The Golden Gong*, by the way? I want Sarah and the girls to read it. Then, with your permission, I'll keep it in my desk for a few weeks.'

'You're hatching something, Mark Nolan,' Dorothy suggested, with a happy smile. 'In a moment, you'll put your head on one side and say quietly: "I have my contacts."'

'And I have. This time it's Eddie Lombard. I'm going to wait till he settles into his directorship and Duncan is safely adrift on the grouse moors, then I'm going to do a Panie Bracie on him: take him to lunch at Simpson's and slip *The Golden Gong* under his nose. He may buy it, he may not. Either way, he needn't know anything about your interview with the one-armed bandit.'

'Mark, you're a living marvel. Everything you've ever done has turned out right.'

'Don't book your holidays on the strength of it. Stick to Mary Orchard, at any rate for the time being.'

'OK. When will I hear from the queen of the silent screen?'

'Olivia Kingsley-Beaumont? As soon as she's finished at Frederick Muller.'

*   *   *

While she waited, Dorothy spent a lot of time at the school-room window, unable to settle to anything of consequence. Her thoughts often strayed to Ida Prince. The erstwhile lovers had said they would correspond, but in the event no letters or telephone calls were ever exchanged. The break was complete. Ida smiled and shook her head in disbelief when she looked back at her infatuation, whilst Dorothy recoiled in disgust from the recollection that she had loved a common prostitute, kissing and fondling a woman who had been used by innumerable men. Such was her inexperience of life beyond the window that she was unable to believe that any man, Robin included, had paid Ida or any other woman to spank him and order him about. Indeed, the further the past receded, the less convinced Dorothy became that her husband had enjoyed the cruelties and indignities she had heaped upon him. She knew the definition of masochism, but she could no more credit its existence than she could deny the sadism from which she had derived her keenest sexual pleasure.

'When all's said and done, I only have Ida's word that he liked it,' she mused, looking down with indifference at what was taking place outside her front door. 'What happened when I had him across my knee was probably due to nothing more than his wriggling about.'

A 1932 Delage, magnificent in deep-shine scarlet with cream mudguards and chromium that shone like maundy silver, was beneath her open window, with Oswald Kingsley-Beaumont (born Higgins) at the wheel and Olivia descending. The hood was folded flat in deference to a balmy November morning. Oswald, languidly self-possessed in cavalry twill, Hush Puppies, white Irish lawn shirt and RAF cravat, his dyed hair delicately waved, was asking his wife if she had forgotten anything. In French. It was that kind of household.

'*Je te dirai ce soir ce qui se passe,*' she replied, for all who had ears. '*Ce sera une drôle de journée, sans doute, qui nous donnera à parler avec nos copains.*'

'*Espérons que Madame Blanchard est au moins civilisée. Bonne chance, ma chère.*'

'*Bonne route! Monsieur Nolan disait qu'elle a beaucoup soufert, mais je ne sais pas de quoi.*'

'*Des gueules de bois peut-être.*'

'*Tout est possible. A ce soir. Sois prudent sur la route, mon clou.*'

Dorothy opened her door to the newcomer with a curt 'Good morning' and led the way to the schoolroom after a perfunctory exchange of names. She had in mind to assure Olivia Kingsley-Beaumont, in French and with the considerable virulence at her command, that she *was* civilised and did not suffer from hangovers; but Olivia's smile appeased her and she soon discovered that it was the visible token of a friendly and accommodating disposition.

A fluent talker who nevertheless knew when to hold her tongue, Olivia was small, neatly made and quick to take charge if occasion demanded. Dorothy guessed her age at fifty-five. Her colour was high, the eyes blue and alert, the hair grey and wiry. She wore a trim blue suit, a frilly georgette blouse and medium-heeled shoes in white-and-navy leather.

Once seated at Ida's desk, she praised everything that came within her compass – the schoolroom, so big and sunny, the background murmur of traffic along Oratory Road, the fragrance of the tea over which she observed Dorothy's stifled agitation and sought to relieve it. Olivia was a chameleon. Capable of assessing people on sight, she immediately adapted to them.

'We're making a start, are we?' she said, cosily, when it was clear that Dorothy was poised to begin dictation.

Olivia worked from ten till twelve and two till four, five days a week, but for most of that time she simply sat and waited, watching with deepening sympathy the writer who could no longer write.

'Don't you have a prompt, dear?' she coaxed, after Dorothy had been tongue-tied for most of one afternoon. 'I'm sure the name Felicity Hatna means something to you. She was very popular when I was at school and sometimes she stayed with us at Pangbourne. I can see her now, in the summer house, writing with a list of characters propped up in front of her. She told us that if she couldn't get started, she would open her husband's cigar box and inhale the scent of tobacco. Nine times out of ten, it triggered her creativity.'

Impervious to the suggestion, Dorothy tried again to dictate. The words came grudgingly, one at a time, and she became increasingly embarrassed as her thin and fatuous material refused to take shape.

'I don't know what's the matter with me,' she sighed, in desperation, having stumbled to yet another halt. 'For years, the rubbish poured out, morning after morning, but now . . .'

Mystified, she slowly shook her head.

'You've got what we call writer's block,' Olivia diagnosed, conclusively, and with a sprightliness that suggested it was an experience not to be missed by the discerning. 'You're in *very* good company, Mrs Blanchard. Even Graham Greene has it, and quite regularly too, yet consider *his* output!'

The days wore on, with little to show for the hours the women spent facing each other. Olivia talked entertainingly about her schooldays in Cheltenham, about encounters with Imogen Holst and Bernard Shaw, about children, pets, travel, the Nolans – about anything she could think of to fill the silent gaps and perhaps break the deadlock. When she failed to persuade Dorothy to lunch with her on Dorothy's birthday, the eleventh of December, she returned at two o'clock all but hidden behind an armload of irises and hyacinths.

'Can you believe, darling, that she only got one birthday card?' she asked perfumed Oswald. 'One lonely little card. And she didn't stand it up anywhere. It lay flat on her desk for days, and just when I'd decided to have a peek at who sent it, it vanished. She didn't seem to find it at all unusual to get just one card. Odd isn't the word for her. When I invited her to spend Christmas with us, she was positively panic-stricken. Darling, I don't know what else I can do for her.'

'Darling, why not leave her alone? Isn't that clearly what she wants?'

'But, darling, she's a sick woman. You may be right, by the way, about the hangovers. I smelt it on her breath yesterday.'

'How does her book come along?'

'I don't think she'll finish it and neither does Mark. Every now and then, the poor thing looks at the row of Mary Orchard books next to her desk and it's as if she's saying to herself: "How did I ever write them?" Darling, the woman is tormented by something and, whatever it is, it's blocking her ability to carry on churning out "the trash", as she calls it.'

'Her husband left her, didn't he?'

'He cleared off with her secretary. But I don't think it's love or longing that's chewing away at her. I doubt if she's ever had more than the most superficial feeling for anyone in her life.'

'D'you suppose she's being blackmailed? According to Ruth, there were rumours afloat at one time that she was lesbian. Ask the Nolans when they're here on Sunday.'

'Saturday. But, darling, we can't pop a question like that. It's no concern of ours anyhow, except I fear she might do something silly – I mean permanently silly – unless someone identifies the problem and lifts it from her brow. Mark will ask about her, of course, and things may flow on from that. But client confidentiality are his middle names, *n'est-ce pas?*'

As it happened, the Nolans mentioned neither Dorothy nor Hilary Blanchard, despite the recent appearance of *Mitten's Luck* to sparkling reviews and climbing sales. It was the literary critic, A. J. C. Villiers, when he brought a copy of the novel to the Kingsley-Beaumonts' Thames-side house (perfumed Oswald called it a villa) who mentioned in passing that Hilary Blanchard was Mary Orchard's daughter.

'Arthur guessed correctly that my husband might be interested in snapping up the television rights,' Olivia explained, still busy with the news when she arrived for work on the Monday morning. 'We had a rather hectic weekend, beginning with a cocktail party for my niece and her husband, but I

133

still found time to do my homework, as it were, before coming here today. *Mitten's Luck* is outstanding, Mrs Blanchard. Arthur has chosen it for his Featured Novel next Sunday and he says he'll rank it with *Bonjour Tristesse*. Here's your mail, my dear. I met the postman at the bottom of the steps. On the hall table?'

Dorothy's nod was scarcely perceptible. Without make-up and wearing an old smut-black frock, she looked paler and more withdrawn than Olivia had yet seen her. Among her letters was a manuscript.

'I've put a fire in the drawing room,' she muttered, lifelessly. 'We'll try to work in there today. I'd like to make an immediate start.'

'Is it inspiration, Mrs Blanchard? I do hope so!' Olivia said; and for the first time Dorothy detected pity in the woman's voice. 'Where did we leave off on Friday? Ah, yes! I have it here. "Sandra and Bev had been into town and bought themselves jeans and white tops to be ready for the school disco".'

Dorothy, her eyes closed, sat in silence for a few moments, then looked into the fire and began to dictate. By lunchtime, she had made more progress than on any previous morning.

'It's obviously from you, Mrs Blanchard, that your daughter gets her creative gift,' Olivia declared, heartily, when putting on her outdoor things. 'I don't know if you recall the enormous success Colin Wilson had with *The Outsider*? That one book made him a celebrity overnight, and there is every sign that *Mitten's Luck* will do likewise for Hilary. Now, my dear, is there anything I can bring back for you? I'll be calling at Harrods on my way in.'

She returned in jubilant mood, having found a copy of *Mitten's Luck* in the last of the several West End bookshops she had scoured.

'It was their very last copy. I want it to give to my niece to take back to Canada, you understand. A second impression will be in the shops at the end of the week, but that's too late because Jean and Paul are leaving tomorrow. My dear, oughtn't you to rest?'

'I'm all right,' Dorothy murmured.

She had slept on the sofa during Olivia's absence, but sleep had neither banished her listlessness nor sustained the morning's fertility. As the afternoon drew to a close, with not one word committed to paper, she silently accepted that Mary Orchard was written out.

'There's always tomorrow, Mrs Blanchard,' Olivia assured her, with great kindness. 'Meanwhile, you have your daughter's success to gladden and encourage you. How proud you must be of her! I don't think there's any doubt that she'll win the GEMA and –'

'Get out.'

'I beg your pardon?'

'Get out of my house,' Dorothy shouted. 'Get out before I murder you.'

The women rose as one. Alarmed by the frightening emptiness she saw in Dorothy's eyes, Olivia made a blind grab for her handbag.

'I believe you would. Take my advice and see your doctor,' she said, tremulously, backing off before suddenly turning tail.

She snatched her mac and scarf as she passed through the hall and looked back once at Dorothy before yanking the front door open, stepping outside, and slamming it behind her.

CHAPTER TWELVE

For the second time that day, Dorothy sank down onto the drawing room sofa, slid her court shoes off by rubbing one against the other, brought her legs up with the knees bent, and buried her face in a cushion. She began to cry, her sobs deepening and gradually subsiding as she drifted into sleep.

It was the long, heavy sleep of mental and physical exhaustion. When at last she awoke, only firelight lit the room. Without shoes, she went to the window and closed the velvet curtains before switching on a reading lamp and fetching the mail from the hall table.

Perched on the edge of an armchair, she opened the large padded envelope and drew out the manuscript of *The Golden Gong*. In her letter of rejection, the agent said that the writing was 'attractive', but the background and period made her unsure of the novel's commercial success. Also, there were no nice people in it.

'Are there any in life?' Dorothy asked, bitterly.

She got up to fetch a knife from the kitchen with which to open her letters, and on her way to the door tossed the manuscript onto the polished table. It struck a package, cannoned off it and hit the carpet with a flop.

Dorothy switched the ceiling-light on and advanced, mystified, on the package. She picked it up and used her thumb to open the striped paper wrapping. Inside was Olivia's copy of *Mitten's Luck*.

Instantly alive, Dorothy flung it with all her force at the fire. It thudded into the hearth, sending poker, brush and tongs skittering this way and that like disturbed rats. Dorothy followed briskly, dropping to her knees on the rug. There, with her mouth a vicious line and firelight reflected in her eyes, she wrenched the book asunder and thrust the pieces into the flames.

* * *

She started drinking in the afternoon, curled up on the schoolroom sofa in front of the hissing gas fire, watching the tongues of flame playing inside the pipeclay flutes.

'I only have to turn it off, let it cool, turn it on again and forget to light it,' she told herself. Then, aloud: 'Headline: "Mary Orchard and Dorothy Henderson in Suicide Tryst. Early Deaths of Writer Who Was and Writer Who Wasn't".'

Another sip. Dorothy licked her lips.

'Want to know my epitaph?' she called out. '"Gone, Finished, Forgotten". That's Dotty's epitaph. I've had my good times and I've had my bad, and after today I'll have neither. It's all over. They've gone away and left me – alone in a haunted house, where all the doors are open and all the rooms empty of people.'

Never again would she stop whatever she was doing to listen to Hilary playing 'La Berceuse' from the *Dolly Suite* on the Bechstein that was now closed and silent. Never again would Ida charm her to laughter with her impressions of people who came to the house. Never again would she hear Robin singing above the rumble of the washing machine, and never again would Panie Bracie 'warn in' that he was coming to town next day and would she feed and quarter him? She and Max had liked one another on sight. Always a moment had come when they had held each other's eyes until she had demurely lowered hers. Had Norah noticed? Was perceived fondness responsible, in part at any rate, for the older woman's hostility towards her?

The telephone rang.

'I'm out,' she called, over her shoulder. 'That's the third time today you've called and I'm still out. Permanently out. I know who you are. There's only one person left in the world who cares if Dotty lives or dies. But I still haven't got a Mary Orchard for you, Mark, so no use to keep ringing me up. No booky for Marky and never going to be. Sorry, Marky.'

Dorothy was drinking neat gin, unaware of the custom of diluting it.

'Thank you, Auntie, for forgetting your bottle. Dotty found it tucked away in your wardrobe,' she continued, aloud. 'That's what you and Rabbit used to call me behind my back, isn't it? Dotty. There wasn't much Dotty didn't know about, but you managed to conceal the boozing from her. Mother's Ruin, they call gin, don't they? Not a bad title for a novel. But of course, old horse, there'd have to be nice people in it.'

Dorothy rose, glass in hand, and started striding up and down the schoolroom in stockinged feet, taking a little gin at each about-turn and calling out some of the comments made by literary agents when returning *The Golden Gong*.

" 'There are, we feel, too many similarities between your Sanderlins and Cynthia Justin Bourn's Lampeters." "I am impressed by the roundness and individuality of your characters, but unhappy with the world of antimacassars and after-dinner billiards that you clearly find satisfying." "*The Golden Gong* lacks pace and is short on suspense – otherwise, I think it a competent first novel." "We like the smooth and logical development of your story, but find your dialogue stilted." To hell with the lot of you! Hear me?' Dorothy shouted. 'Some of you can't even spell or afford a new typewriter ribbon. Well, I don't need you where I'm going.'

She bumped into her desk, staggered before steadying herself, and put her drained glass down. Then she unpinned her hair so that it fell to her shoulders. She walked to the window, stopping within a yard of her reflection.

'Know who I am?' she asked it, archly. 'Dotty Henderson, the Wild Woman of Willow Square. I was dotty enough to imagine that by Easter I'd be living in France, with *The Golden Gong* selling well and a second novel coming along nicely. I was looking forward to a life of silence and solitude. Those are the second and third of Dotty's priorities, you know. They are heavenly when she can write. They are unbearable when she can't. That's all I have to say to you at the moment.'

More gin. She closed one eye and looked up at the ceiling-light through her glass.

'Who was it said alcohol is the anaesthetic that enables us to undergo the operation of living?' she demanded. 'Was it Winston Churchill or Mickey Mouse?'

She returned unsteadily to the window, breathed on the

pane and wrote MM in the mist. It was dark outside now and snowing.

'All the little people coming home from work. Look at them!' she muttered, contemptuously. 'I do think nice people are so important, don't you? In a novel, I mean. *Wuthering Heights* is full of them and *Crime and Punishment* is positively overflowing. And here, bless my soul, comes the nicest of them all. Marky. Marky in a big white Cadillac. And he's seen me.'

Dorothy drew back, remembered the lights and hurriedly switched them off, bumping into this and upsetting that in her haste. Then, as Mark began ringing the bell, she went down one floor and to the head of the stairs, where she crouched in the darkness like a child who has crept out of bed to listen to a party going on below.

'Dotty's got nothing for you, my love,' she said, mournfully, when Mark changed to using the knocker. 'Dotty's done what she said she'd never do, Marky. She's let you down.'

She put her arms round the newel post and rested her head against it, closing her eyes and murmuring that all she wanted now was sleep, sleep, sleep. But Mark, shouting through the letter flap, kept pulling her back.

What was Mark saying? Oh, it was coming from such a long way off, echoing through tunnels and chambers and endless passages. Something about Eddie. Eddie. Eddie who? And why was it urgent?

EDDIE!

Suddenly alert, like a dog at the sound of his master's return, Dorothy listened intently, scrambled to her feet and listened again. From beyond the front door came the cough of a starting engine.

'Mark! MARK! Mark, wait for me!'

Dorothy ran down the stairs, her frock filling with air, until nylon slipped on wool and she pitched forward. Her body hit the black and white tiles with such a slap that it might have been dropped horizontally from the topmost landing. The last thing she saw, as blood entered her mouth, was Mark's visiting card, and the last thing she heard was the swish through soft snow of his departing car.